# Oh, Henry

Joanne Alain Cook

JACBooks

Dedicated to Bob and Sparky

# Prologue

alking down that hall, I felt my chest constrict sharply, my breath shorten, and the blood drain toward my legs. *Flight, flight, flight.* That was what my body wanted from me. But it was too late, I was already there and was now obligated to look.

*Don't be another dead body*, I pleaded to the Gods of fate.

But the Gods rarely listened to me.

# Before

Henry

Despite my desperate wish on an evening star, I seemed destined to suffer through the dog days of summer in solitude, watching real canines and people play in the distance. That curious hobby had been ignited by a dog park opposite my new home, which was conveniently framed in the large front window for my viewing pleasure. I observed that park while sipping my morning coffee, while shuffling through my midday mail, while stretching before my afternoon yoga, and while sitting aimlessly in the evenings, all alone. My eyes drifted naturally to those people and dogs every day, and the watching made me feel connected to them.

An old friend once accused me of becoming an introvert and at risk of becoming a social nitwit. Not my fault, a failed engagement and several years of intense schooling created my terrible loner tendencies. Long nights preparing for complex exams, like the NAPLEX, and little else left me socially strange. I now found myself slightly anxious around normal interactions with a confusing urge to connect with people and avoid them at the same time. So, I began a side career of people watching and dog watching to balance my innards, and it worked. I now felt like a substantial part of those people and their dogs, but at a distance, of course, from behind my window, while wearing a special gemstone to combat anxiety.

Honestly, though, at first, seeing those large animals nudged me to purchase a big can of pepper spray, and I carried that can religiously for one full week after moving into my home. Fearful images flashed behind my eyes, graphic images, of a large dog jumping me outside my door. I imagined it would happen as I set off on my walk to work and cause me to run late, something unheard of, me being late. Anticipating such an event, I would whip out my can of high-intensity spray and shoo away the offending animal with a steady stream of aerosol spice, and then waltz right into work on time.

But that fearsome event never occurred. Those dogs and their people always behaved very nicely. They kept to their side of the street, only sending waves and good mornings to my side. So, after that first week, my high-octane pepper spray ended up on the narrow wall-table near my front door, forgotten.

The dog park resembled a caged green expanse of trimmed field, broken up by a long strip of crushed granite, that might be used as an emergency runway for a small radio-controlled airplane. Dogs often frolicked up and down that strip and the flying tennis balls soared and landed and bounced. A black dog caught every ball before it touched the ground, a

Labrador. He would leap high into the air and just hang for a moment until a ball magically found its way into his wide-open mouth. That black dog always arrived with a very nicely structured man. A man that bore a striking resemblance to the near shirtless duke on the cover of an interesting novel I recently picked up at the CSV book counter, the type of novel I often yearned to pick up but never dared to purchase before. My eyes always to drifted to that man, because he played with his dogs as carefree as a boy, and moved in a harmonious dance with every canine that ran up to greet him.

Each day, familiar people strung familiar dogs into the dog park, or maybe it was the other way around, perhaps the dogs strung the people along. Or, maybe it was both. It was surprising that I found dogs and their people so fascinating. In the past, I always considered dogs gross, dirty and slobbery, but these dogs and their owners were now my community, my friends, my people.

I'd only spoken to one of those dog people in the short month I'd lived across the street, the old lady with the white fluff dog. But that encounter didn't occur in the dog park or out on the street. We spoke in the CSV pharmacy, and in a professional, no-nonsense voice, I explained the side effects of the prescription drugs scattered between us. I studied her through a window, another safety glass partition keeping me isolated from the real world, which struck me as funny, because my summer job in the pharmacy was supposed to be my chance to experience life in the real world, the world away from books, and classes, and term papers.

I'd always been a bit shy, but my severe aloofness kicked into high gear following the death of my father. His passing left me alone in the world, and I regressed into myself. My mind pointedly focused on completing a college degree and mastering the challenging science and math subjects that led to medical school and my lofty lifelong dreams of following in the deep footsteps of my dead parents. My personality narrowed to revolve around numbers and calculations. I gravitated toward people who never wasted time with silly small talk, and who never bothered to stare deeply into my eyes and guess how alone the world had left me. I realized being alone was a trivial matter because we were all really alone in the greater scheme of things. But sometimes I wished it wasn't so.

I preferred men to be neat and clean, intelligent like my father had been, aloof and responsible, and maybe a little goofy. I actually got engaged for one day, to a man even more regressed than myself. After my father died, we spent two years *dating* before our short engagement. Those dates had consisted of marathon study sessions with delivered dinners while we each read different textbooks, capped off by no-nonsense, austere, stress relieving sex. Nothing about our relationship was messy. We connected on a very high intellectual level but lacked the physical sensuality I read about in classic fictional novels, the passionate nonsense. *It's fiction*, I'd told myself.

The most romantic moment in our history happened on a beautiful summer day in the park as we hurried from the library to find another closed room in which to study. We shared a single ice cream cone because we lacked the spare change for two and dallied next to a duck pond quenching our dry palates. I admitted that he had a valid point, but it spoiled the mood. *So what* if it was very unhygienic, what we were doing in the park with that ice cream cone near those curious ducks. And now, I didn't kid myself, I realized that I am very unskilled at normal romantic banter.

But my destiny might change soon, and my wish might manifest in a true love story, because I met someone after recently moving to Sacramento. Someone who might be in search of a romantic adventure, like myself. I met a potential mate, an appropriate man, and he comes across as quite a normal person, who considers me fairly normal, too. And he already romanced me a little bit, like in those fictional novels.

I met Josh at the convention center during the pharmaceutical sales conference exactly one week after moving into my little house. He worked for Biogentech, in sales. There was no mistaking that red and white DNA stenciled on his name tag, *Josh Butler*, as he stumbled to the last seat in the dining area during the lunch break. That chair hid in a corner of the room behind a small table meant to be obscured by a plastic plant and facing me in my social anxiety haven.

He flustered apologetically as he transferred his armful of papers, food, and sloshing liquid onto the table. His hair stuck straight up in a neat crop cut, and I perked up at the sight of him, a tall, handsome man with a pharma job and a romantic name, Josh Butler. At least, it appeared romantic written in script above the curvy graphically drawn DNA. All sorts of dreamy ideas rushed through my head because I really pined for a summer romance, wished for one desperately. Josh holding out a chair for me, Josh holding open a door, Josh climbing up a tall tower to rescue me, all with his clean shirt tucked tightly into his trousers.

"Sorry, I just need to set this down for a moment and readjust my grip," he muttered and then did a double take of my wide open curious eyes.

I hardly ever had the nerve to speak to strangers at conventions, but Josh began chatting to me like we were old friends. Then, he plopped down in that last empty seat because I was smiling at him with all my teeth. It was too late to be aloof now, my googly eyes had already come out. Josh Butler turned out to be very friendly and easy to talk to. He drew in all of my attention, which was great, because I was trying to ignore the bulk of the room. When we discovered we both lived in the greater Sacramento area, we made a dinner date, causing me to believe I wasn't such a social introvert after all. All it took was changing my environment and smiling unabashedly at a stranger.

Our first date went just as well as our first meeting despite me being a social introvert. Josh was oblivious to my shyness. He talked on and on about his office, and his brothers, and the paddleboard he recently purchased. He had other conventions to attend soon, one in Texas, the other in LA, one in Japan if he was lucky. He happened to be a traveling pharma salesman.

He gazed into my eyes when he spoke and only glanced fleetingly at my dress and my east coast cashmere sweater. I could not tell if he liked what he saw, but he kept up the conversation easily. I smiled when he smiled. I laughed when he laughed. Then came a startling silence right before the check arrived. I worried that he may have finally realized that I hadn't said a word.

"'I'm sorry I talk so much." He leaned across the table, worried. "People tell me I talk too much. I'm a blabbermouth and I get a little nervous. I talk when I'm nervous, and I think you are so fantastic."

*What exactly did he find so fantastic,* I wondered. I was not sure he knew anything about me except that I recently completed pharmacy school and moved to Sacramento, didn't have any local friends, and laughed agreeably at odd times during his banter. I admit, I mostly admired him for nothing other than the fact that he kept talking so insistently and because he was very neat and truly cute, with a romantic name. Cute counted for something because it had been a long time since a cute, tall, guy flashed his eyes at me like that. Maybe I missed it because my nose had been buried too deep into schoolbooks. But now that my schooling was on pause while I worked my sample job, I had time to focus on a cute Josh Butler type and a possible romance.

"I enjoy your banter," I told him shyly, and he smiled, much cuter than any of the washed-out fellows in the pharmacy program by a long shot.

When Josh dropped me off after our first date, he was delighted to see the dog park. His eyes lit up with anticipation.

"You didn't tell me you lived right across from an exercise park," he beamed. "Maybe I can bring Henry some time."

Then, Josh dropped in with Henry the hound two days later, and again the next day, and the next, and the next. I never had such a romantic, attentive beau. He didn't want to study or brood about equations; he wanted to kiss and talk about the sunset and spy on the dog walkers with me. He brought me little treats and flowers, but I wasn't fooled, a big part of my allure was that dog park. Josh could kill two birds with one stone. Get a little *girl* attention and exercise his hound. He always left his dog in the park to join me on the other side of the living room window, and we watched Henry the hound from afar as we kissed and cuddled innocently.

Josh pointed to random dogs and told me their names but that information went in one ear and right out the other. I was too focused on having a real romance, maybe even a steamy romance, and I hardly listened. I recently began reading a thick paperback book, a non-classic novel, and realized a true romance might involve a bit of scandalous passion. If a book could elicit certain feelings inside of me, I should expect normal courting would, too.

But after two weeks of visits from Josh and Henry, I had to admit to myself that Josh might only be a terrific new friend and nothing more. We just weren't physically right together, not like *Maggie and the duke* in that book. Our kisses felt too chaste, too lukewarm, and never progressed into anything uncontrollable. Josh never left me *gasping for breath* or *aching for more*. The correct course of action entailed breaking it off with Josh, and I sat absorbed in my thoughts, dreaming up a way to tell him without hurting his feelings.

"So, what do you think about that?" Josh smiled nicely.

"What? I…Yes, good, I guess. Fine."

I had a terrible habit of pretending like I heard things and then acting agreeable out of embarrassment. I failed to ask for clarification because Josh had a way of prattling on and on about whatever it was, the playoffs, the governor, the latest blockbuster action flick, and if I agreed, he rewarded me with a nice pause in the babbling. He did the same this time, nodding like he found me completely awesome. Perhaps I would wait another day or so to break it off with him. *Or maybe not.* It was nice having someone to sit on the sofa and spy out the window with, and maybe those lukewarm kisses needed more time to simmer into something warmer. Mainly, I didn't feel like such a social nitwit with him coming around so often.

Two days later, Josh returned to my door with Henry on a leash and a "baby" bag filled with Henry's overnight necessities. In my lackadaisical dismissal of Josh's babbling, I inadvertently agreed to babysit Henry for almost two weeks. Josh ferried in a large doggie bed and placed it right smack dab in the center of the den and grinned at me.

"Or maybe you want him to sleep in your room?" Josh's eyes grew wide with anticipation.

Perhaps he imagined if I agreed to Henry sleeping in my room, I would agree to Josh sleeping in my room. Good grief, it was entirely too soon for such decisions. Our kissing had not even passed the smooching stage yet, and *that* decision should be made in the heat of an activity that made it impossible for me to say no, shouldn't it?

"He might be less homesick in there, where he can watch you sleep. He likes watching people sleep."

"Doesn't he sleep outside on a dog house?" In my mind, a distinct image of a canine snoozing on top of a red doghouse materialized, lying on his back, big black nose in the air, perfectly happy, with a little yellow bird for a best friend.

"Oh no." Josh laughed, not falling for my little joke. "Henry is an inside dog. Henry," Josh took the large, wrinkled face with the big floppy ears into his hands, "you'll be staying with Sarah for a little while. Be a nice house guest, just like you are for Stan, okay? I'm saying please."

Then, he placed a food and water dish on the kitchen floor and thoughtfully moved my mini-potted olive tree outside the sliding glass door, banished to the wild.

"We don't want to give Henry any ideas," Josh chuckled.

*What ideas?* But he couldn't stay and chat. Josh needed to check into the Sacramento International Airport and catch a flight to Japan. He owed me big time, he grinned. He loved that he could count on me in a pinch and believed ours was a relationship destined to last. *Oh my.* He passed a handwritten instruction list for Henry's care, dramatically dipped and kissed me in the deepest kiss of our short history, then skipped down the walk toward his sparkling convertible Lexus sports car.

# Day One

## with Henry

Henry was a bloodhound with a wrinkled brow and sad, woeful eyes. He must have lived through something serious. A terrible war? A lost love? Failed puppyhood dreams? Or maybe his pathos resulted from being very quiet and shy and antisocial most of his life. Maybe Henry hadn't experienced a real romance yet. I completely related to him. On his last visit, Henry hadn't been keen on frolicking with the other dogs in the park. He discovered a hidden spot under a bench and stayed socially cautious, an introvert. He sniffed around solo while glancing at the other dogs. I saw his curious eyes watch the fetching game, tracking the tennis balls, but not daring to catch one.

Now, alone with only me, he shook out large floppy ears and settled his tannish, darkish body to lounge in front of my sofa. He emitted an easygoing air and barely moved when the door closed behind Josh's departure. *Just let him sniff around the dog park for an hour and he'll be grand,* Josh wrote on his instructions sheet. *Let him stay out longer if he acts out.* I reclined against the cushiony rolled arm of my sofa as Henry steadily watched me read. *And so, the tables had turned,* who was watching who. His front paws stretched out under his large nose as he stared from under hooded eyes. Good grief, a steady stream of drool dribbled from each corner of his mouth. My colorful, adorable area rug became darkened by the river of moisture seeping from his doggy lips, creating an enormous wet spot on my yoga space.

"Oh, Henry, maybe you shouldn't drool so much," I suggested softly. "It isn't polite."

Henry could care less about being polite and continued drooling on my beautiful rug. Bucket loads.

"I suppose you'll want to visit that dog park across the street," I said.

No response. He just blinked and kept drooling. Good grief, he looked so sad!

The short note on dog care instructions got straight to the point: Let him out in the backyard in the morning to relieve himself. Give him one and a half cups of food, don't let him con you out of more. Give him a few pats on the head and leave him with his squishy for the day. When you get home, feed him, one and a half cups again, then let him run around the dog park for an hour. He should be good until morning but if he needs to go out again, he'll stand by the door and bonk it with his nose. *That's his signal.* He's pretty self-contained, all he needs is a few pats on the head while you watch television. Henry isn't very needy. Kind of like me, right?

At the end of the note, Josh had drawn a big smiley face with large eyes. It was a pretty accurate self-portrait; Josh was a very happy man with a big bright outlook.

I decided to do a little work while Henry drooled on my carpet. He seemed pretty comfortable, and I became curious to see if the drool would stop before dinner or if it would continue into infinity. Would he need to replenish that liquid anytime soon? My work would keep my mind busy as that experiment transpired. I happened to be a temporary pharmacist at the CSV in Natomas, and I decided to update the material safety data sheet binder because my mind was not used to being idle.

When I first surveyed the pharmacy a month ago, many of the tabs were outdated, mostly because the chemicals were no longer in stock and the store had altered their MSDS log to an automated system. But it didn't look good, having outdated material tucked into a drawer, they needed to be categorized better. I didn't say anything at first, but as I became friendly with the lead chemist, I suspected Doctor King might be an overworked old man who had trouble juggling all the small stuff. I offered to update the MSDS reference manual even though it had been hidden in the back drawer destined for the recycling bin. It would be nice to have a hard copy of those safety sheets around. Like books, I preferred paper to digital. What if there was a blackout and an emergency at the same time? We'd want an updated hard copy binder, wouldn't we? Doctor King chuckled, pleased as punch with my enthusiasm, and so I found myself slowly shifting through the files in an old and unneeded binder on my days off.

After an hour of reading through chemical safety sheet warnings, it was time to take a break and do some stretches, but Henry the hound had appropriated the center of my workout area for his prolonged drooling experiment. It occurred to me that Henry could run around the dog park during my yoga stretches. He could take in the fresh air and I could have some privacy for my workout. The dog park had to be more entertaining than watching a woman bend all around the living room.

I fished inside his large overnight bag and found his leash, a large rope with a clasp. Which of the two fat metal loops on his brown collar should I clip it on? Did it matter? As I fumbled with his thick leather collar, Henry lay on the ground ignoring my every move. I patted him on the head, and he flicked his eyes at me for less than one millisecond. *Did he miss Josh?*

"Don't be sad," I told him softly. "He'll be back before you know it. Let me take you across the street. You'll have loads of fun. Don't be so picky out there, and you might just make a friend."

I'd never entered a dog park before. There were two large fence doors separating the dog run from the rest of the world. They each opened into a tall square of cyclone fencing. Immediately after Henry and I entered that small enclosed square, several dogs in the main park gathered around the inner door to bark at us. They also sniffed and jumped excitedly, causing a level of unease to rise in my chest. *Good grief.* If I opened that door, they'd surely run into the small cyclone isolation chamber and continue right out the park. I frantically glanced around and spotted the old lady from the pharmacy staring at me, slowly standing. Had she recognized me with my hair down, wearing body spandex and sweats, and my face free of those small square spectacles?

"Close the outer gate!" the old lady directed with a wave of her hand. "Do not open the inside door until you close the outer gate!"

Of course, that must be the purpose of the isolation chamber. I closed the outer gate before I unhooked Henry's leash and opened the inner door. Several dogs instantly rushed into the chamber and raced all about. I pushed the door wider and tried to shoo them into the dog park, but they jumped and yelped and circled Henry and me. Henry stood politely aloof in the commotion while I pulled my arms in to protect myself. People in the dog park observed the activity without a single move to fetch their dogs. Were they amused? I was addled, not sure what to do. A red-haired man stepped up to the outer fence door with a spotted jumpy dog who yelped at the dogs inside the isolation zone.

"I'd like to come into the park," the man mumbled behind the chain links, holding his dog down.

"Those dogs need to come back in here," the old lady chimed in behind me.

I spun around and waved my hands to urge the dogs into the park. Not one of them paid me any mind. Not even Henry. How exactly did anyone manage to get these dogs to obey? They completely ignored my shooing hands and gentle urges. On the dog park side of the cage, a different man jogged over and held the large gate door wide open. He whistled loudly, and all the dogs stopped moving instantly, even I stood startled, at attention.

"Clover, Bluebell, Mollie!" He threw tennis balls, one after the other, and three dogs scampered after them back toward the crushed granite runway. The man grinned at Henry and held out a neon green cloth-like disk. "Look at this, Henry," he said to the uninterested hound. But when he threw that neon green ring into the park with a sharp *go-get-it*, Henry sprang into action and the rest of the dogs followed close behind. Then, the man held the large chain-linked door wide open for me, smiling with a strong square jaw. I obediently followed his commanding hand and stepped into the dog park. Then, he closed the door for the man with the spotted dog. Good grief, how would I exit the park without any dogs following me? I turned to the man who had thrown all the balls.

Thick, dark brown hair spilled over his ears in an interesting wavy mess. His square jaw appeared to be rough, and the wild growth sprouting out indicated days had passed since it last saw a razor, also interesting. He wore a T-shirt stretched tightly over a broad chest and khaki shorts. I recalled seeing him before. He always threw tennis balls, and his large black dog was an expert at catching those balls in midflight. Up close, his eyes were bright brown orbs surrounded by thick lashes, and his smile divine. I was not sure what just happened, but I felt a sigh deep inside, a fluttering. Was it because he had rescued me from several beasts when I was trapped inside a chain-linked cage?

"I'm Matt," he managed just before the dogs returned and gathered around him. He held out large hands to accept the returned slobbery balls and could hold all three tennis balls in one hand, easily. Then, he threw them out in a high arc, one by one, and the three Labradors ran off. He wiped his now slobbery hand on his long shorts, along the sides and on the rear, over what appeared to be a nice and tight gluteus muscle. Typically, I'd find the slobbery mess totally odious, but an odd urge to assist him overcame me. I had to stop myself from reaching over to wipe sludge off the back of his shorts. My goodness, I felt an instant physical attraction to him. This man was nothing like the neat, intellectual, nerdy men I was used to. He appeared to be a solid mass of sleek muscles with a handsome face on top, and his eyes stared right at me.

"Hi, I'm Sarah," I said meekly, but I wasn't sure he heard me.

By now, the man with the spotted dog had shut the inner gate, and his large Dalmatian ran off in a sprint down the granite runway. The two men greeted each other loudly as I receded into the background. I began to slowly slink away, toward the cage door for my escape, when a loud voice, deep and piercing, froze me in my tracks. The old woman from the pharmacy had her hands on her hips, and her eyes bore into me.

"Oh, no, you don't!" Her angry voice grew louder with each syllable. "You are *not* dropping off your dog and leaving."

*Loxaprine, Zoloft, and Zaleplon,* flashed into my head. Those pills were not for her, she had informed me in a similar deep voice. She picked up for folks in the retirement community right down the street, she's a med runner. She often helps the older tenants, and so I should get used to seeing her, Jane Bennet. Her relationship with Doctor King went way back, and he always made sure her pickups went smoothly, without delay. Fragile old people counted on her. She had picked up for a woman named Elizabeth Lavenza. In the dog park, at the moment, Mrs. Bennet did not appear to recognize me from the pharmacy. With my long hair loose, and those small square work spectacles tucked into my white lab coat pocket, sometimes I didn't recognize myself. Granted, in the pharmacy, the old woman had barely glanced at my face, annoyed that I was not Doctor King.

"You and your boyfriend have been leaving that hound dog in here without supervision. That is a major dog park faux pas. Major!" The old woman admonished me loudly with a pained expression. "Your boyfriend thinks he's slick and charming, he thinks he's funny. But this behavior cannot go on. You cannot leave an animal unsupervised in the dog park. Don't think I won't call animal control and have him picked up."

"Oh hey, Mrs. Bennet." Gallant Matt stepped closer, but the other man, the red-headed one with the spotted dog, moved away with an amused smirk on his face.

"It's the law." Mrs. Bennet was neither intimidated by muscles nor wooed by pretty eyes. Obviously, Matt's attention did not cause her legs to quiver like jello, that effect must only be limited to my limbs.

"She's across the street?" Matt defended me. "It's not a big deal."

"You should take those boisterous ones to the other end. Away from the entrance." Mrs. Bennet indicated the jumpy dogs gathered around him. He tossed the tennis balls back down the runway, then rubbed the slobber on his tight rear muscle again. She continued, "And it *is* a big deal. We can't go making exceptions for every pretty face that walks in here. Yesterday afternoon, everyone agreed the next time Henry came over, we'd lay down the law."

At that moment, a rather stooped brown dog appeared at her heels.

"Oh, now, Old Major," Mrs. Bennet peered down at the old dog. "I wasn't calling you. You can go back to your shade." Her eyes darted to an old man sitting in the shade of a small tree. Then, Mrs. Bennet patted the old dog on the head. "Okay, I'll give you a special treat, in a moment." She yelled over to the old man. "I'm going to give Old Major a treat!" The old man answered by raising his hand momentarily, then Mrs. Bennet resumed her stance to admonish me. "You may not leave your dog in the park unattended. There are rules to be followed. If the rules aren't followed, chaos will commence. I don't mean to be harsh, but that fellow of yours refused to listen to the rules. He thinks being across the street is close enough. It isn't. I must tell you, I found your fellow a mite bit rude."

"I… I'm sorry," I stuttered. A plethora of eyes stared at me, and I felt like shrinking. I did not enjoy undivided attention or confrontation. I kept myself faced away from the two men, embarrassed, and focused on Mrs. Bennet's beautiful paisley scarf. She was a plump woman, short but very colorful. "I wasn't aware of that rule. I'm so sorry. Henry is not my dog, and I'm only watching him. I never owned a dog before, and I don't know the rules of the dog park. Of course, I would never intentionally break a rule. I'm absolutely mortified."

Her eyes relaxed, and she insisted I not worry about it. She suspected it was all Josh's doing. She invited me over to the bench she had been sitting on. Her little fluff ball of a dog stood alert on that bench, tracking our progress. She gathered up the small white dog while making cooing noises that sounded ridiculous, then plopped onto the wrought iron bench with a heavy sigh. The dusty dog she had addressed as Old Major followed slowly and sat nicely at her feet. Another dog sprinted over to sit next to Old Major, in the same pose, and I sank onto the bench opposite the old woman, feeling much like I might be in the principal's office. Mrs. Bennet reached into her bag and pulled out a clear plastic container of treats.

"Here you go, you old dog." She passed Old Major a dog treat. He instantly took it and hobbled slowly away, tail wagging sporadically.

"And you too, Mollie." The other dog's tail thumped vigorously at the treat. She was a beautiful golden dog with flowing locks.

"Hey! Hey!" A petite woman jogged down the granite runway toward us. I knew something about this woman from my previous people-watching days. She often did bench pushups, jumping jacks, and other such exercises in the dog park, and she jogged outside the fence, circling the dog park two days ago. I had wondered if we could be friends. She looked about my age, twenty-six or so. Her dark hair was tied back in a high tight ponytail, and her chin was very sharp. "I asked you not to give Mollie treats! Come on, Mollie! Drop it!" She nodded once at me, then gave Mrs. Bennet a bit of a glare as she urged her golden retriever away.

"She looks starved for attention." Mrs. Bennet chuckled after them. Then, the old lady stroked her furry white pooch and held it up in display. "This lovely little boy is Snowball. Isn't he absolutely adorable? Snowball, this is the one responsible for Henry. Miss ..."

"Sarah," I said, "Sarah Fitzgerald. I live right across the street."

"Everyone knows where you live." Her nose wrinkled up. "We also know Henry doesn't live with you. But that dog's been in here more often than you or that young man of yours. He ignored me the last time he dropped Henry in the park, and you need to tell him about the rules." She tapped her little dog's nose and hissed. The little white fluff immediately sat stone-still, gazing up at her. "No, Snowball, those treats are not for you. Let me fetch yours."

"I wasn't aware of the rules. I'm not sure, I don't think Josh realized-"

"He realized," she cut me off. She waved her chunky hand around, indicating the two men further down the granite runway, the two who were at the gate a moment ago. "Watch out with those two," she warned. "They also *bend* the rules, and their dogs certainly reflect their bad behavior. Bingo is very jumpy, and he's a Dalmatian! Stella and Bluebell have lapsed in their behavior, too, ever since Lola left them in her brother's care. You may find Matt to be easy on the eyes but take my word for it, he's a deadbeat. Irresponsible, that one. I don't think he's washed those two Labs yet." She nodded, affirming her own words. "He's house sitting and dog sitting. He doesn't have a home of his own and is mooching off his sister, a disciplined woman. I believe she's been deployed overseas for a few months. And her dogs are growing spoilt and unruly, and he's plain lazy. That other one, George, he's also a deadbeat. Only rides that fancy bicycle around. Thinks he's going to win the Tour de France someday." She let out a little snort.

I glanced at the men she referred to and caught them looking at us, and they quickly turned away. Somehow, it felt like everyone in the park might be staring at us, yet not one set of eyes were facing our way. That sharp chinned woman was doing jumping jacks again, others were talking, and the two men from the gate were focused on the jumpy dogs chasing balls. Those two rule-breakers were both dressed very casually and looked in good shape. George had short reddish hair and wore tight Lycra shorts, while Matt's longish hair, messy with wavy strands, fluttered in the breeze. I was not sure why my eyes were so drawn to Matt in his messy shorts and T-shirt. I did not like messy, but he was a good-looking man with a strong, solid frame and boyish energy, and *he had been looking at me!* He stood casually, calmly, and his arms were distinctly cut so that I could pick out his triceps, and biceps, and his brachioradialis sections even from the distance. Good grief, those large hands could hold four tennis balls at the same time!

"Poop!" Mrs. Bennet stood up. She pointed with a short stubby arm and hand, tipped with an extended finger for extra effect. "Poop!"

The Dalmatian who entered the park with George had paused in his ball fetching to relieve himself behind the men. Both fellows turned toward the spotted dog squatting in the grass, straining. George spun back to Mrs. Bennet with a sour expression.

"Keep your shorts on," he called over. "He's not even finished."

"That's another rule," Mrs. Bennet huffed. "Do not leave poo! When that fellow of yours left his dog in here unsupervised, he also left the poo! That is a major no-no. Major no-no! I'm not sure you realize how incredibly large a no-no it is, leaving the poo."

Across the park in the shade, the dusty Old Major perked up momentarily. The old woman glanced at that old dog from the corner of her eye. She ran her hands over the white fluff ball in her lap and spread her legs further apart. Her plump thighs were almost the size of my waist. She must have bleached her hair snow white to match her dog, a thin sliver of grey sparkled against her head. Was she trying to channel Cruella de Ville? But her eyes were nice and soft powder blue orbs of innocence, and my inner meter could not decide if she was friend or foe.

"I'm aware Henry isn't your dog, but today, I take it, he's your responsibility." Mrs. Bennet pinched Snowflake on the nose and cooed again. "If Henry drops a bomb, there is a container over there. It's filled with plastic bags from the grocery store. I'm certain Henry is going to drop a bomb. All big dogs do, marking their territory, and Henry dropped one every day your fellow left him in here, it's natural. But don't leave it again. You can have your fellow come in here and pick it up when he comes by later. I'd like to see him finally pick up after his dog."

My eyes shot to Henry. *Don't drop a bomb*, I pleaded silently.

"Oh, now look at that."

Mrs. Bennet indicated Old Major. A smaller dog snuck up to sniff at Old Major. The old dog scooted away, but the younger dog persisted in sniffing at him.

"Poor old soul. He's too old and in too much pain. Wait for it."

Suddenly, the old dog snapped violently at the young pup and the younger dog ran off.

"He's getting snippy in his old age and is going to hurt someone one of these days. That old man didn't even notice that snip. He tried to bite someone just last week," Mrs. Bennet grumbled. "There aren't many rules around here but it's proper etiquette to follow them. Dogs should not bite, or hump, or jump up on people. No leaving a dog unattended in the park. Pay attention to your dog and correct bad behavior, not like old Joe over there. Pick up all of your poop, immediately. It's the right thing to do, it really is. Looks like Henry is doing his poo."

*Good grief, no!* Henry squatted in the grass about halfway down the run with a long excretion coming out his backend. I cringed, *Please stop*!

But for once, Henry did not look so sad. He actually appeared to be grinning at me. His hooded eyes settled right on me. *Ha, ha, come pick up my poo*, his eyes said. I desperately wished for that box of latex gloves sitting on my desk at work.

"That's a two-hander." Mrs. Bennet laughed. "When will your fellow be coming back?"

"Not till next week," I mumbled.

Nothing about picking up dog poop felt like the right thing to do. I glanced everywhere for a sink and soap dispenser, someplace to wash up after completing such a task. All I could see was a water fountain with a low spigot over a water dish. That red headed man across the way, George, stooped down and used a bag over his hand to retrieve his dog's poop. I felt a strong rebellious streak coming on. This was not on the *take care of Henry* note! There was nothing about picking up dog poop on Josh's handwritten slip of instructions.

I watched as red-headed George carried his ominous bag across the park and threw it into the metal trash can, then he went right back to his ball-throwing spot, pausing to shake hands with the old man sitting near Old Major. *Good lord*, he shook hands without washing them first! I glanced at Mrs.

Bennet in horror. Her light blue eyes wore a serious look of concern.

"Next week you say?"

I wobbled to a stand, anxious and upset, biting my lower lip. I stared at the plastic bag container wanting to run home and be a rule breaker for the first time in my life. I did not want to pick up dog poop.

"Maybe you need a little help," Mrs. Bennet spoke softly and stood up next to me.

Was she going to help me pick up the poop? But Mrs. Bennet directed her attention to the baseball diamond on the other side of the dog fence, where four boys on the pitcher's mound hit baseballs against the backdrop. Mrs. Bennet raised her hand in a wave, and one of the boys perked up. He dropped his bat and ran around to the dog park entrance. That boy was a skinny, tanned, dark-haired smiler. Mrs. Bennet turned her light blue eyes back to me.

"Micah," she told me. "He takes odd jobs. He'll help you with Henry if you tip him. He'll pick up the poop for you. This one is on me."

Suddenly, Micah was there, smiling and glancing between Mrs. Bennet and me. He looked about eleven or twelve years old with dark tanned skin and bright happy eyes. Before I knew it, Micah grabbed a plastic bag and skipped out to where Mrs. Bennet indicated, behind that small tree about three feet into the grass. Micah scooped up the heavy load and delivered it to the trash can, he turned on the low spigot, and several dogs ran over to take turns under the water flow. Micah giggled and ran off. I turned to Mrs. Bennet.

"You're my hero," I said simply. I wouldn't be surprised if a tear was in my eye.

"Stick with me on things." She nodded to me. "And you'll be fine. Beware of the deadbeats and rule breakers, they'll lead you astray." *Definitely, a friend.*

It took me twenty minutes to collect Henry and leave the dog park. He lay in the shade, not moving a muscle, for over an hour until I approached with the leash. Then, he suddenly decided to run away from me and lay in a different spot. He ran away at my every approach. Most of the folks in the park watched me chase him unsuccessfully. One of the deadbeats, red-headed George, snickered. The cuter deadbeat probably would have laughed, too, but he had already left with his obedient chocolate and black-colored dogs. After I gave up and walked sulkily toward the gate, Henry trotted up behind me, panting near my ankles. His doleful eyes smirked, *Just kidding.*

Back home, I wondered where to put his bed for the night. I maneuvered his padded sleeper to the top of the damp area rug, but Henry dragged it into the hallway instead, trying to get into my bedroom. I closed the door on that idea. Henry seemed determined to block most of the walkway right outside my bedroom. In the end, I let him have his way. Then, we ate dinner. I measured out his dry food and poured it into the dog dish, round crunchy pellets of food that he woofed down before I could sit at the table with my plate. I endured melancholy eyes that made me feel guilty for eating chicken and rice with stir-fried vegetables while he had already finished. Josh's note clearly said not to let Henry con me out of more food, and I stood my ground on that. Okay, I did offer him some of my extra chicken and rice. That dog food had looked so dry, and he had lost a ton of fluid with his drooling experiment earlier. When I turned in, I could hear Henry breathing heavily in the hallway. I never closed the inside doors in my house and didn't realize his breathing would carry through the halls so effectively. It took hours to get used to his sounds, and I fell asleep much later than usual.

# Day Two

## with Henry

My alarm felt extremely early and I resisted opening my eyes. Then, I noticed the heavy panting, and my heart catapulted into high gear. *Good grief, what was that?* Then I remembered Henry. Henry lay just down the hall, breathing loudly with his raspy doggy breath, keeping me from falling asleep and now waking me up. But his loud rasping sounded close, too close. My eyes flew open and I turned to find Henry lying in bed with me. He gazed at me from under his heavy droopy brow, lounging casually on top of the covers, waiting for me to awake, drooling again. *This was not exactly what I meant in my recurring wish to wake to the sight of mouthwatering eyes staring intently into mine.* All those wishes wasted. I should have been more specific.

I jumped out of bed. But Henry just lay calmly watching me.

"Up, up!" I urged. But Henry just lay calmly watching me.

"Let's go, go!" I motioned vigorously. But Henry just lay calmly watching me.

"Out!" I pointed sternly to the door. But Henry just lay calmly watching me with his deep hooded, oh so sad, puppy dog eyes. Maybe he didn't understand English.

Fine, I decided to ignore him. Who needed to make a bed anyway? I stumbled into the bathroom to brush my teeth and wash my face. When I wiped my eyes I noticed my audience, Henry, at the door watching me, drooling all over the bathroom floor.

"Henry! Has anyone ever told you it's rude to stare at someone in the bathroom?"

But I stopped myself. Didn't I watch Henry the day before, going to the bathroom? Good grief, was this tit for tat? Henry opened his jaws wide and yawned enormously, bored with me, then he turned and left me alone to finish my morning routine. I quickly tied my hair up before following Henry's paw prints into the kitchen.

There he stood, bonking his nose on the glass door to the back patio. That was his signal! I opened the door and

Henry padded right out and sniffed around the yard. He chose a spot and peed. He sauntered back inside and stood expectantly next to his water and food dish. I measured out his breakfast, then I poured myself a bowl of dry cereal so we could stand side by side crunching together next to the kitchen slider door. Eventually, Henry found his way back into the front room to my now dry area rug. I patted his head as he gazed up at me. Then, I left for work wondering why I had been so apprehensive the day before. Taking care of this dog was going to be a snap.

*Erythropoietin, 800mg Motrin, hydrocodone,* George Wickham's medications were not in the system. Doctor King and I converged in the back room and examined the handwritten prescription from a doctor in the downtown common's office. A landline phone was pressed against Doctor King's ear as he spoke into the receiver. Doctor King inquired why Mr. Wickham's medications were not showing in the system yet. I peeked out the door to where red-headed George lounged against the pickup counter. He barely glanced at me when he had come in, and now he flirted shamelessly with Cathy Nixon, one of the daytime cashiers. His sunglasses sat on the top of his head like a tiara. He wore a bright red and yellow shirt with a different pair of tight Lycra shorts, cycling attire.

"Cycling is a total lifestyle, if you're serious about training." His voice carried around the shelves and filtered into the small office.

I half listened to two conversations at once, Doctor King on the phone, and George flirting with a married mother of two.

"You can't be serious about training if you're split between obligations."

"He brought in a handwritten note, dated yesterday morning, but I don't see a record in the system," Doctor King repeated.

"I need a partner who understands that riding takes one hundred and ten percent of my time. A woman who knows what it takes to be a champion, to make a champion. A girl who will allow me to be her champion, it's a partnership." The voice from around the corner.

"Can you simply ask the doctor if he wrote this prescription?" Doctor King asked.

"Modern women, a real modern woman would understand. Let's be honest here, a man is just a boy that needs to compete, right? Men are boys that need to show off for our women. I'd surrender to being a peacock for the right woman. Just call me a feminist," George insisted.

"Okay, okay, no need to call him at home. Just check if this patient is in your system at least. It's our first time seeing him here," Doctor King explained.

"Believe me, I agree that women are the stronger sex, and I can definitely step aside and let a woman run the show as long as I can train properly. I need to find the right woman." George's voice had gone soft, quiet.

"I see. Okay, we can settle this up tomorrow," Doctor King said.

"A man can't concentrate if he's worried about paying bills…" George's voice had trailed off. Perhaps Cathy Nixon walked away. I spied out the door. Yes, Cathy had turned her back to George and searched in the distance in an attempt to move away from him without appearing rude.

Doctor King cradled the phone, shaking his head. His eyes squinted at the vault, the locked cabinet system we used due to the street popularity of some of the drugs it stored. He blew a steady stream of air out his lips and peered over his thick glasses.

"Go ahead and fill the 800 milligrams Motrin, but he'll need to return for the rest of this order tomorrow afternoon or later. You can tell him there's a little backlog, or whatever you want. It'll give his order time to show up in the system. Doctor Achilles is notoriously forgetful. His prescriptions are always a day late, it's outrageous. Hopefully, he returns our call later today or as soon as he gets in tomorrow morning." Doctor King rubbed his eyes. "To do things by the book, we need to have it in the system. I admit we sometimes just fill them, because the system always catches up, especially from *that* office. But we'll do everything in the correct order until you're settled. It's only a minor delay for this gentleman."

I returned to the pickup window, and George strolled over with a bright expression in his eyes. His brow creased minutely as he took in my face. *Did he finally recognize me?* People seldom remembered me because I was always very quiet and had a very average appearance. Frizzy brown hair, unremarkable eyes, basic body usually hidden under very conservative wardrobe choices, and I rarely wore jewelry or make-up. Only, with the dry heat in California, my appearance had changed subtly. My hair fell in a much tamer straight line, and the sun had added surprising red-gold highlights to my head, and my slight glowing tan teased out the subtle green of my eyes that I thought was lost in childhood. All added together, I might actually have become a tiny bit pretty on the west coast. But I was still quiet. I passed him a bottle of twenty tablets of 800mg Motrin and watched his brow crease even more.

"I'm very sorry, sir, but we won't have the erythropoietin, or the hydrocodone available until late tomorrow at the soonest. You might want to call before coming in to confirm we have the order ready. I'm very sorry for the inconvenience."

"That's crazy," George spat out. "My regular pharmacy fills this on the same day!"

"I'm sorry, but I'm unable to fill these medications at the moment. You're welcome to take the prescription to your regular place if you need it right away."

George stared at my face. His nearly transparent blue eyes bore right through my glasses and into my own eyes. He glanced over my hair and neck, and I knew he recognized me. He broke out in a huge grin.

"You're Mrs. Bennet's new friend!" He chuckled. "From the dog park. You're the girl from across the street with the big hound dog. Hi. I'm George, spotted Dalmatian, we met yesterday, entering the park. So, you're a pharmacist."

George leaned generously over the counter and placed his hands between us, crossing under the glass line and violating my space. His smile morphed into a devilish crease with one side turned up more dramatically than the other. He shifted slowly from foot to foot and rubbed his reddish, brown crew cut. Was this flirting? *Deadbeats and rule breakers,* Mrs. Bennet's voice echoed in my ear.

"Yes, hello, I'm Sarah," I said softly. "It's nice to meet you again."

"Wow, you're young. I mean, usually, pharmacists are old men, right? When they said someone new started here, I never dreamed it would be a pretty girl." His eyes creased as he glanced at the Motrin. He thumped the counter with his finger. "No problem about this, Sarah, I completely understand. I can take that prescription to my regular place.

I'll get it all there. I need this stuff for training purposes, you know. No worries, I'll get it filled somewhere else."

He reached across the counter and retrieved the square prescription paper, then buried it behind his back, likely in that back zip pocket on his shirt. He kept his handsome grin aimed at me the entire time.

"I'm so sorry about the delay. If you want, I can add your information into our system, it might help the order clear faster for next time. We'd have a record of your normal prescriptions and can keep a running order."

"Oh, no, no need for that." He shook his head. "I usually use another pharmacy. I just stopped in here for something else and thought, why not try the CSV pharmacy, but it's totally okay. I'll go to my regular place. No worries."

Then, he began a retreat, slowly backing away, grinning and waving. He bumped right into the next customer, excused himself, gave me another glance, then exited quickly. George Wickham? Jane Bennet? *For real?* My own name, Sarah Fitzgerald, made me feel like I had dropped into the wrong romance novel. Thank goodness the next customer had a normal name, Kathleen Smith.

My mind would not let it go, and I mused all day about the strange coincidence of names, George Wickham and Jane Bennet. I wondered where that cute Matt fellow fell into that scheme of things. I racked my brains trying to remember if a Matthew character was in that novel? Maybe Matt was his middle name and the cute fellow's first name was really... *What was Mr. Darcy's first name?* It wasn't Matt, that much I knew. *What if cute Matt's last name was Darcy?* Wouldn't that be crazy? My own name was Sarah *Elizabeth* Fitzgerald. Maybe I was meant to be Elizabeth! Now I was curious to learn the names of all the folks in that dog park. Perhaps I had entered into an alternate reality and that fictional story was coming to life. Perhaps my wish for a true summer romance was manifesting itself in the real world. Good grief, was this fate? Chills ran down my spine thinking about it. I needed to get a copy of *Pride and Prejudice* and read it again, right after I finished that other book.

I hurried briskly down the jogging path that paralleled the levee. I always walked to and from work because I didn't have a car, it's how I got my nice light tan. I avoided buying a car because I was still undecided about my future. Would I stay in California and go back into academia, or would I stay in the real world? At the end of the jogging path, I turned the corner and noticed the practically empty dog park, just the old man and dusty Old Major sitting in the shade. Another hour would pass before the afternoon strollers filtered in. I felt a buzz of anticipation. I could barely wait to fetch Henry and zip right over. My social anxiety must be tapering off if I couldn't wait to meet people. I might finally be emerging from my *move across the country where everyone is a stranger* funk!

I slipped into the front door, smiling a mile wide, searching for Henry, my ticket into the dog park. We loners would help each other make friends in that dog park. We'd break down our personal barriers and embark on new and exciting social adventures. Maybe we would become part of a summer romance before my life got busy again. There he was, right where I left him. Henry barely moved a muscle at my entrance, he just raised his overlarge head at me. Translation, that's his excited hello! I sat down and patted his head and massaged his thick folds. He liked that! His tail moved back and forth. We were communicating, connecting. Then, I noticed a faint pungent aroma in the air. A little like ammonia and musty cloth. Wet dog? But the dog wasn't wet.

The aroma wafted from the corner of the room where the carpet appeared dark with dampness. I moved closer to inspect it. Did he drool in the corner? I noticed the other corner of the room next to the sofa, dark and damp. Good grief, I sniffed. Was that urine? My jaw dropped at Henry, but he just pointed his nose to another corner of the room, an uncarpeted corner where a thin yellow film covered the ground. I quickly inspected the house and found evidence in every corner of every room. *Yuck! Crap! What the hell!* Did he need to pee in every corner of every room? I steamed back into the living room toward that drooling, slobbering monster who lounged on my now wet and offensive favorite area rug. I felt the tears threatening to burst. I felt extremely violated and furious. *Well, that was a very quick romance, Henry.*

I was just about to scream at that carefree hound when it hit me. The poor dog had been trapped inside the house all day and needed to pee. I had imprisoned him in my tiny home, and he had needed to pee but couldn't get out to relieve himself. His eyes blinked at me, so woeful. He probably fought with all his might to hold it in and couldn't. He probably only allowed little bits out here and there, hoping not to make a big mess. That must be why he did it in the corners. He didn't want to pee all over the entire floor. Poor Henry. Poor, sad, trapped Henry! He blinked at me again.

"Oh, Henry, do you need to go out?" I walked quickly through the kitchen to the back glass door and pushed it wide.

Henry followed me. He waltzed right out back and went to the far corner of the yard where he let out a long and steady stream of yellow. He must have been holding it in painfully all day, which meant there really was a monster here, me. Geez, what was I supposed to do? Maybe I should have come home during lunch and let him out. Why didn't I think of that earlier? I never even gave a thought to Henry and his natural needs.

I left the slider door wide open and pulled out the baking soda and vinegar. I started with the carpets, hoping to erase any stains and the smell. Henry must be totally embarrassed. The vinyl floors were easier. Mr. Clean should work fine. I went from room to room, corner to corner. *Good grief!* Henry hit every open corner of the house. He surely thought he was being considerate. As I scrubbed the last corner of my bedroom, Henry wandered in to supervise my progress. His sad eyes blinked at me, and the corner of his mouth drooled with another slobbery mess to wipe up, but I didn't flinch. Was it really that poor fellow's fault he had a little accident? Who was the monster here?

"I'm sorry, Henry," I muttered softly. "I didn't think it through. Josh's note implied you only needed to pee in the morning and the evening. But you're not a robot, are you? And when nature calls... " I reached over and kneaded his brow. "Next time, just let a big one go in one spot, like in the spare bathtub maybe, or on one of the linoleum floors. Or I'll come home at lunch to let you out. I wish I had a car now. Maybe I'll get a bicycle."

Henry's tail wagged happily, and I was forgiven.

"Let's go to the dog park," I said.

We were old pros at getting through the cyclone cage this time, now that we knew what to expect. I took care not to throw the fence doors wide and opened it a small crack to only allow Henry through, then I followed him in. At the far end of the granite run, I spotted Matt and George right away. They were both staring at me as I closed the gate, and each raised a hand in a wave. I quickly waved back, elated, then looked away. But not before I noticed Matt stood a hair taller and was broader in the shoulders than George. I briefly worried if Matt was also looking for a modern woman to support him. Mrs. Bennet did call him a deadbeat. Henry meandered to his favorite shady spot, and Mrs. Bennet sat in her usual spot with two other women. She waved vigorously at me, and I strolled to them.

"This is the young girl I was telling you about," Mrs. Bennet spoke loudly to the women sitting in her circle. "She's taking care of Henry and has never owned a dog before. It's not her fault he was left in the park all alone."

"Hello," I stepped up to the small group. "My name is Sarah."

"This is Caroline and Isabella." Mrs. Bennet made the introductions. They were both petite and looked in their thirties or forties, Caroline with long blonde hair, Isabella with short dark hair. Caroline wore Capri jeans with a loose top and Isabella wore shorts and a tank top.

*Caroline, there was a Caroline in the story wasn't there?* I quickly glanced at Matt with the wavy hair. He threw three balls at once and all the dogs jumped for joy. *Wouldn't it be something if his last name was Darcy?* I turned back and shook hands with the two ladies. I noticed Mrs. Bennet studying me. Goodness, did she finally recognize me? I had forgotten to let my hair down. I smiled at her and joined them.

"Oh," Mrs. Bennet tilted her head at me. "You look like the new pharmacist at CSV. You are so transformed with your hair up!"

I chuckled in confession.

One of the women had worked at CSV for a short time, as a cashier. She was well acquainted with both Cathy Nixon and Doctor King. Caroline owned the yellow Lab, Gatsby, chasing balls at the other end of the park with Matt's chocolate and black dogs. Her husband Eric usually brought the lab, but he was doing yard work, so here she was. The other woman, Isabella, owned the mixed shepherd with the white socks and patches named Rosie, and at the moment, Rosie was in a chasing match with the golden retriever Mollie. Mollie's owner Grace, the girl with the dark ponytail and sharp chin, was at the other end of the park doing bench pushups between jumping jacks. Clearly, Mrs. Bennet's circle did not approve of Grace.

"She hardly pays attention to Mollie. That's why Mollie is always out of control. She lets her dog jump on people and beg anyone who enters the park. Disgusting," Mrs. Bennet said. "Plus, rumor has it, she had a scandalous affair that broke up her marriage. The poor dog became collateral damage in that relationship."

"She gets incensed when Gail gives her dog a treat." Isabella rolled her eyes.

"I only give the poor dear a treat because I feel sorry for her," Mrs. Bennet chuckled. "Look at them over there. She likely has poor Mollie on a strict diet, too. I'll bet Mollie doesn't get anything nice. She deserves a treat now and then."

Their prattle volleyed back and forth as they scathingly critiqued each of the owners and each of the dogs. Soon, the fetching Labradors and the Dalmatian joined in the game of chase with Mollie and the shepherd. Every dog vied for the same neon green floppy disc. To my silent joy, Matt and George slowly inched their way toward my side of the dog park. Matt wore a different T-shirt, torn at the bottom, with cargo shorts and some type of strap-on sandals. Matt's hands went up to scratch his jaw, and I noticed his messy whiskers were missing. If he shaved, he must not be a deadbeat. Shaving suggested he went to a job earlier? Perhaps Mrs. Bennet's constant venom was just old woman vitriol. The three women tittered quietly as the men drew closer.

"I'm just saying," Mrs. Bennet smirked softly, "if you're going to wear shorts like that in public, people might have a thing or two to say about things."

Surely, she meant the tight bicycle shorts on George. The women completely hushed their talk when Matt reached the water fountain dog spigot and turned it on with his brachioradialis flexing nicely. The sight of his muscles made me warmer than Josh's kisses, I noted. He tipped off the two large dog dishes, then let the water flow for the Labs. Every dog wanted his lips on that spigot. Matt stuck his hand in the water, then splashed and rubbed the back of his neck. He glanced over and caught me observing him. He flashed a large, white, gorgeous smile at me and stood tall. He must be used to women eyeing him.

"Hi, ladies." He moved toward us but got diverted by the jumpy dogs.

When I glanced back at my circle of women, it was clear each of them noticed I had been ogling Matt. I certainly hoped the heat in my cheeks wasn't showing. I tried to play it off by casually asking a question. It was the only question on my mind, so I blurted it out.

"Why does Caroline keep calling you Gail? Is that your middle name, or your preferred name?" I asked Mrs. Bennet. "Isn't your name actually Jane?"

Caroline's confused eyes flicked between Mrs. Bennet and me. Mrs. Bennet threw her head back and chuckled, looking a little embarrassed. Then, she leaned in as if telling us all a deep, dark, amusing secret.

"My name *is* Gail. The Jane name is a joke. That old doctor you work with, Doctor King, always calls me Jane for some reason. I never like to correct him, so everyone calls me Jane Bennet at the CSV, and that's who they have on file to do the med-runs. I don't have any prescriptions of my own, I'm just the pickup gal. I don't know why he chose Jane to put on that roster. It happened a long while back, and now it's kind of stuck."

"That's so funny," Isabella said.

How unusual. Doctor King did not seem like the sort to confuse a name or make one up. He was a stickler for accuracy. I wondered if Gail Bennet's identification was on file in the system. But my musings were interrupted by Matt and his naked forearms. He decided to join our circle and stood a few feet away with his white teeth flashing, waving his large hands scandalously in front of me. Good grief, his eyes were bright, light brown, and shiny like the tiger's eye mineral. Asbestos flashed into my mind. I once read asbestos in tiger's eyes gave it that reflective shine, heat resistant, fire-resistant asbestos, but hazardous to your health. I clutched my gemstone necklace. It had a nice smooth teardrop shape that calmed me in such situations.

"How is it going with Henry?" Gail asked. "Shall I send Micah to help you out sometime?"

"Oh," I confessed. "I made a major blunder today. I feel very bad about it. I'm not sure how to manage Henry during the day. Josh's note said I could just leave him with a squishy and he'd be okay for six to eight hours, but I can see how gullible I was. It appears he had to pee sometime during the day but I locked him up in the house, and he didn't have a place to do his business."

"He had an accident?" Gail and her two friends nodded sympathetically. "I bet it was quite a puddle. Did he at least do it by the door? Big dogs should be able to hold it. Did you spank him?"

Spank him? For a little accident? I shook my head. "No, no. He was trying to be polite about it. He actually held most of it in, and he did it out of the way, in a few different corners. I think he was ashamed that he couldn't hold it." I nodded at their puzzled expressions. "I think he tried to make as little mess as possible, doing a little here and a little there, trying to hide it."

"In more than one corner?" Gail Bennet wore a sour expression on her face.

They each chuckled. Good grief, what was this? All heads turned toward Henry the hound, who stood up under their scrutiny. Henry stuck his huge tongue out and shook out his ears. Then, he turned to the entrance where a nice-looking older man and a boxy black Labrador with a red collar closed the inner gate.

"Your dog was marking his territory," Gail said, then noticed the man at the gate. "Oh now, wait a minute!" She jumped up from her seat to take a few stomping steps toward the gate.

I glanced at Matt and caught him staring at me with his shiny golden eyes. I felt myself blushing.

"Marking his territory?"

Matt shrugged his shoulders and spoke in a hushed voice. "It happens. Dish soap, salt, and vinegar usually works on rugs. Leave him outside tomorrow, in the backyard, or he might do it again. If he marked his territory and thinks he got away with it, he will do it again."

"You mean outside? Isn't it too hot?"

"He'll be okay. Just leave out a big dish of water."

But the commotion Gail instigated with the new arrival drew everyone's attention. The old woman stood half that man's height, but with her hands on her hips and her feet spread out, she created a massive barrier. The man stood with his arms across his chest, barely glancing at her.

"You let that animal swim in the canal again, didn't you?" Her pointy finger flicked the air like a knife. "He stinks to high heaven! Who knows what diseases he's bringing into the dog park. And there's a law about letting your dog off the leash. Don't you care about that?"

The older man gave Gail Bennet the once over and grimaced. His black Labrador trotted up to give him a tennis ball and the man threw it back onto the granite. Soon, Matt's black and chocolate Labs joined the wet dog and all three Labs began chasing each other.

"I'm calling animal control, I warned you." Gail Bennet stalked back to her bench with a cell phone stuck to her ear. She glared at Matt. "Don't you say a word. He's not supposed to let that dog off the leash, even up on the canal. Only men can't follow the rules!" she snapped. "Now it stinks to high heaven in here! That filthy dog better not touch my snowball."

"Labs are water dogs. They love to swim." The man spoke loudly towards Gail "He isn't hurting anyone by swimming on his walk. If you're concerned about your little dog, you should take him to the small dog park. It's right over there. You won't have to put up with the big dog play. That side of the fence might be more your speed."

"Snowball thinks he's a big dog. He gets his feelings hurt over there."

The man snorted a laugh and walked a few steps further away. He threw a purple tennis ball for the dogs, and all three Labs scrambled in a competition to capture it.

Matt flashed a closed-lipped smile at me before departing to join the newcomer. The two men shook hands and turned their attention to the Labs frolicking on the granite runway. They walked down the dog run, putting ample distance between their fetching game and our wrought iron benches. George, at the far end of the field, moved to meet them. Matt glanced back at me briefly, and I had the distinct urge to jump up and follow them. But that would put me in with the rule breakers and deadbeats, a place I had never been, with the naughty kids. Gail, Isabelle, and Caroline all glared in the direction of those Labs and the deadbeats.

"Oh, now, look at that," Gail griped. "That kid's mother is going to be spitting mad."

A small boy, who had been throwing a ball for a charcoal-colored dog with a fluffy white tail, ran across the granite to pat the trio of Labs on the head. The wet black Lab shook his entire body and little droplets flew through the air. The boy squealed with delight. The men offered him tennis balls, and the boy threw each one by placing them in a bright plastic ball launcher for more leverage. The Labs and his fluffy-tailed dog all scrambled to retrieve them.

"They're over there now," Caroline said softly. "The stink's going away, problem solved."

"I'm still requesting someone come out here immediately. I bet he keeps that dog outside with a stink like that. It's criminal behavior and dog abuse." Gail's eyes narrowed. "He needs a ticket, or a warning, or something at the very least." Gail fidgeted in her seat. "This is how we lose a nice dog park. Allow chaos. Allow rule breakers. Allow bad behavior. I'll not stand for it. Hello?" She turned her head and spoke into the phone, muffling her voice.

Caroline and Isabella sat rigidly, staring silently at Gail, and I wasn't sure if they also felt diffident about that phone call. Was Mrs. Bennet causing trouble or reporting trouble? *Friend or foe?* Plenty of signs in the park, along the canal walk, and near the playground requested owners "keep dogs leashed", and one sign listed a fine. Matt, George, and the new man were chatting nicely, and no one besides our little group on the bench seemed upset by the wet dog at all. I'd watched that man and dog plenty of times while walking home from work. They often strolled on top of the levy, the black Lab running freely, chasing rabbits and waterfowl with abandon. Up until Gail Bennet's outburst, I never thought anything of it except, what a happy dog he had.

"Bob Batten," Gail said loudly into the phone. "He let his black Lab off the leash *again*, he let that dog swim in the canal which is hazardous to that dog's health- Yes, at the large dog park. Yes, right now." Gail tapped her finger on the phone with a gleeful gleam in her eye. "They're in the neighborhood. Just wait. I warned him. I warned him plenty of times."

The sun drooped in the fading blue sky. In the west, an orange glow appeared along the bottom of faraway clouds, and in the east, puffy white hats on the mountain tops reached out toward us. It was hard to tell how the beautiful evening would end. Gail Bennet's phone call hung in the air as the squealing boy, Bob, and Matt continued tossing balls for their team of fetchers. That entire group was having a wonderful time. Some tennis balls flew up high, some bounced down low, a few skidded in the loose crushed granite, and the one black Lab jumped and hung in the air magically. Then, the group of canines grew so the chasers also included the golden retriever and George's spotted Dalmatian. The dogs jumped enthusiastically, ran, and play fought over the tennis balls in a glorious dog party. The ladies in my group stared at the action stoically. *Was I in the wrong group?* I shot a look at Henry sitting calmly in his shade. He also watched the dog fetching extravaganza with interest. Then, one of the balls ricocheted off a tree to land right in front of Old Major and the old man sitting on the midfield iron bench. The little boy raced toward Old Major, but the old dog grabbed hold of the ball and hunched down. The boy slapped Old Major on the nose and commanded the dog to *drop it*.

The next few minutes seemed to happen in slow motion. A white animal control van cruised into view on the opposite side of the fence and wobbled to a stop. Old Major dropped the purple ball, and the boy reached down to pick it up. Old Major changed his mind and closed his enormous mouth over the ball and the boy's hand, at which point the boy screamed out notes on the soprano end of the music scale and his eyes became perfectly round. The men, Matt, Bob, and George, sprinted toward the boy and Old Major while Old Major's old owner took two shaky steps backward at their advance. Matt took hold of Old Major and began to pry his jaws open. George hovered near the boy, holding back both his excited spotted dog and the boy's fluffy dog. Bob blocked the jumpy Labs from joining the action with outstretched arms. Old Major's owner wore a disoriented face as the dogs began to bark all around him. Everyone else in the park stood and leaned toward the action, staying away as the animal control fellow came clanging into the park. A skinny bald man, who had been reading under a far tree, moved quickly toward the group yelling out the name *Tommy*. Matt finally pried open Old Major's jaws wide enough so that the boy could recover his hand and the ball, but then those jaws snapped down hard on Matt. His happy sparkly eyes cringed in pain. The skinny man scooped up the little boy and carried him toward the main gate. Bob and George pulled the other dogs a few feet further away and Matt managed to pull his hand out of Old Major's jaw. The animal control guy swooped in and lassoed Old Major with a noose attached to a long pole. The animal control guy jerked the lasso tight and pinned the old dog's head to the ground. Old Major let out a heart-breaking whimper.

"No!" Old Major's old owner sprang forward. "He's just an old dog! He's weak. You can't put that cord around his neck! He didn't mean it!"

Gail Bennet sprinted toward the commotion with her fat arms flying haphazardly and her feet pounding up dust from the granite runway. I felt myself breathing funny and held my arms to my chest. I noticed Caroline suddenly snap a leash on a yellow Labrador and make a beeline for the exit. Isabella closed the space and moved right up next to me.

"That dog is dangerous!" Gail declared to the animal control fellow. "I knew he'd bite someone again. And you just shush up, Joe. You know Old Major's past his time. He's in pain and is a powder keg waiting to happen. If you had any sense at all, you would have taken care of this a long time ago."

The skinny man had taken his boy to the exit gate, he paused to whistle and a small patched dog followed them out of the gate, along with Caroline and her yellow Lab.

"I'm a witness, I'm a witness." Gail's gleeful volume increased. "This dog has been deteriorating and becoming dangerous."

"Hold on there." Bob Batten crouched down petting three different dogs, holding one's collar and another between his legs. His wet dog fidgeted obediently to the side, watching him.

"No!" Gail used a stern and commanding voice. "This nonsense has got to end. That old dog has been in terrible pain for weeks and now he's acting out because of it. I know it. We all know it! Do the right thing, Joe. You're going to be lucky if that father doesn't sue you."

In the end, the animal control man dragged Old Major away in the white van. Bob offered to drive a shaky Joe to the shelter to find out what needed to be done. Gail stomped back to retrieve Snowball, angry that only Old Major had been detained and not any other dog she pointed out. Mrs. Bennet growled that she was going to high tail it to the shelter to make sure the real story didn't get lost "in the nonsense." She hollered around the park, but no one could identify the boy or his skinny father. Although, several people knew the patched dog's name was Biscuit.

The entire incident left me shaky. That had been a very intense shouting match, and I felt unsettled. Henry played his resistance game again, and it took quite a bit of patience to get him to stand and follow me to the fence door. When we finally got there, Matt and George were waiting for me. I could see dried blood on Matt's hand.

"You should clean up that bite immediately," I said. "I have antibiotic right across the street if you'd like to get that taken care of."

"No, no. I can manage it fine. I'm just on the other side of Regency Park. It'll keep for another few minutes." He grinned at me. "We're going to be late if we don't get moving."

"We wanted to invite you to Swabbies," George chimed in. "A few of us go out for fish tacos every other week. They have live music, outside, by the river."

"Seriously, now we've got something to talk about." Matt chuckled. "No really, just a few of the lower-key folks. Grace, she owns Mollie the retriever, myself, George, sometimes Bob and Joe, and Dave, he wasn't here today but will be there, and Mike and Minni sometimes come. Just casual dog park buddies without the queen bee. Come out and get to know the lighter side of the park." He smiled with his big bright teeth, and I smiled back automatically. "No pressure. We usually meet around six and stay till at least nine, if you're interested. Swabbies on the river."

Was I interested? Oh my goodness, yes! The lighter side of the park? The rule breakers and the deadbeats had to be more fun than Gail Bennet and her posse. Cuter, anyway. And Mrs. Bennet acted very strange. If she was such a stickler for rules, why did she allow Doctor King to insert the wrong name for her in the CSV system? Surely, she realized it was highly irregular, even illegal, to give a false name to a pharmacist? Maybe Doctor King got it wrong, but she should have corrected him.

The invitation teased me all the way to my front door. Should I venture out to socialize on a work night? Would it be irresponsible to meet a group I barely knew on the spur of the moment? I did need to eat, and I did want to find out the gossip on what was happening with Old Major. And then there were those golden-brown eyes, with the muscular tan forearms connected to those very large hands, and that body that resembled a duke! *I still need to find out Matt's last name.* I shut Henry out on the back patio with his food and water and called an uber. Fish tacos, how could anyone say no to fish tacos?

Swabbies reminded me of an outdoor beach bar, the type that lined the sandy ocean expanses in Florida. But there was barely a beach, and no ocean, just a fast-flowing river. I spied it through the leaves of valley oak trees as I moved through the parking lot. From my vantage point, I noticed the outdoor bar was decorated with several life-size wooden pirate statues and numerous old picnic tables of different shapes and sizes. Everything looked weatherworn. I passed eight large motorcycles, all Harley-Davidsons, parked just outside the entrance. There was a small cover charge, but I was already covered. The tank topped hostess glanced up at me and smiled.

"Sarah the pharmacist?" She asked.

"How did you know?"

"Dark eyebrows with lovely brown hair, greenish eyes, about five foot seven with a chunky blue rock on a silver chain around her neck. Beautiful face, smart looking, and classy sexy."

Good grief, is that how they described me? Beautiful? Sexy? Who said that? *Please say, Matt!* I looked around, suddenly worried she meant someone behind me, then grabbed my chunk of purple and white lepidolite. I often wore that stone to combat my anxiety. That mineral was riddled with the element lithium, and though I would not ingest such things to help me cope, I had no problem wearing them in copious quantities.

"Was it the necklace that gave me away?"

She laughed and laughed with me. Well, if I had been laughing, it would have been with me. Then, she reached over and banded my wrist. She directed me to the outside seating area where a cover band played ancient rock songs. I spotted the dog park crew right away. They took up two tables in the middle of the open area. Swabbies was not crowded, and I let out a little sigh of relief. The people were a tad older than the downtown scene Josh had taken me to on one of our two dates. The Swabbies crowd exuded a more relaxed vibe, and many people wore tee shirts, shorts, or jeans. I needed to accumulate a less formal wardrobe. My palazzo pants and silk blouse did not fit in with the casual outdoor bar. George spotted me first and ran right over to escort me to the table.

"Hey! Doc! You came!" He grinned. His red hair glowed crimson in the late evening light.

I strolled to the table, glanced at everyone, and waved. Matt wore a button-down shirt, clean and pressed, and obviously used gel in his wild hair. He gave me a little nod. I also recognized Grace Briar, her ponytail had disappeared, but her chin was still sharp. Surprisingly, Caroline sat across from Bob and a woman who must be his wife by their proximity, her name was Joanne. There was another couple I often spied from my window, Mike and Minni Wilson, and they owned a Great Dane. Caroline greeted me with bright eyes and seemed more relaxed than she had in the dog park. She made the introductions. I sat at the end of the table, closer to Grace, Matt and George. They shared a pitcher of something on the table, and George used an empty glass to offer me some of the drink.

"It's a Squabaritta. You'll love it." He winked.

"Thank you." I accepted the drink. Grace raised her eyebrow at him, and George turned away from her. Matt smiled and clinked my glass. "Thank you to whoever took care of my cover charge," I added.

"My pleasure," George twisted back around and slid down next to me. His pale blue eyes were not wavering. "Do you ride? I'm a cyclist. In training. I have a UCI ranking. I've been on two world tours. I was an alternate for the postal team last year, almost. Do you follow cycling at all?"

I chuckled, "No, sorry."

That didn't seem to put him off.

"He's really fast," Matt said. Grace bumped him with her arm.

"He's *superfast*." Grace's eyes flashed darkly. "Hey, Romeo, she has a boyfriend, remember?"

"I'm just talking here." George smiled at her. "Making friendly conversation. I'm not trying to move in on Jeff."

"Josh," I corrected.

"Yes, Josh, of course. *Josh*, my bad." George said.

"So, Josh is out of town for a few days and you're looking after Henry, nice of you." Matt was not drinking the slush drink, instead he sipped a draft beer. "As I said earlier, leave Henry outside, he'll be okay. Dogs can survive outside for a few days. How long is Henry staying with you?"

"Two weeks, roughly, I guess." Too freaking long.

"Wow, that's some business trip. But Josh looked very professional, impressive. We saw him the other day in his suit and tie when he dropped Henry in the park. God, Mrs. Bennet about had an aneurysm when he left Henry again." Grace laughed. "He's quite handsome, your Josh. Where'd you guys meet? College?"

"Oh," I looked at each of them. "No, we met at a drug convention."

"Sounds like fun," George said. "I want to go to a drug convention."

Everyone laughed.

"He's my only friend in Sacramento. We met at the convention center downtown. I've only been in the state for about a month. I'm just, you know, settling in."

They each appeared stunned.

"Well, you have us now," Grace said.

Bob and his wife left the table to dance. That spurred Grace to insist everyone join them, and she immediately dragged George with her to the area in front of the stage. Caroline also meandered toward the dance area. Matt claimed his hand felt too achy and lounged with his beer. He took food and drink orders and said he'd wait for the waitress. I helped by writing things down, and we relayed everything to the waitress when she returned. When a popular metal rock song started, the Wilsons also went off to the dance area, leaving Matt and me to watch the purses and phones alone. We stared across the table at each other, and I wondered if he had described me as beautiful, sexy. I certainly would describe him as beautiful and sexy. I never would have imagined forearm muscles were so eye-catching. The muscled forearms of the cartoon character Popeye popped into my head. Good grief, no wonder Olive Oil was so smitten! I looked down at Matt's bandaged hand.

"I hope you cleaned that wound well."

"I did," he said.

"Does anyone know what happened at the shelter?" I asked. "Did Mrs. Bennet really follow them out there?"

I didn't miss much gossip, Matt told me. Bob did not see Mrs. Bennet at the shelter when he dropped Joe there. He did say that Old Major was not allowed to go home right away. The dog needed to be quarantined a couple of days because Old Major had bitten someone else recently and was considered a repeat offender. Old Joe insisted on staying with his dog, all night if possible, as Old Major was frightened of new places.

"Old Major did not actually bite that boy," Matt insisted, "And my bite was my own fault. Old Major snapped his jaw out of fright and confusion, and because I pried his mouth open. Plus, all those other dogs got him all riled up."

"You should get a tetanus shot, a booster." I told him. "Animal saliva is riddled with bacteria, and it doesn't hurt to be safe."

"I think I'll live," Matt chuckled.

How might I describe this? Our eyes were like opposite sides of a magnet, drawn to each other. We gazed? We stared? We sat mesmerized. At least, I was mesmerized by his eyes. Did I mention they were golden brown, sparkly with thick lashes? We spent a good five minutes not saying anything while I stared at him, and he gazed back with a small smile cracking his lips now and again. For once in my life, I did not feel overtaxed with anxiety. My purple lepidolite was working wonders, and something about Matt created an interesting little quiver in my chest. Just as I had that thought, the silence became deafening. Did he think it was unusual for a strange woman to sit silently and stare at him?

"I can't believe how nice you are. Looking after his dog for a whole week." Matt finally broke the silence. "And you've only known him for what, a month?"

"Almost," I said.

Matt took a swig of his beer. "He's a lucky guy."

"So, what's your last name, Matt? Matt..."

"Diller. Matt Diller. How about you? Sarah, Doctor..."

"Fitzgerald," I told him, slightly disappointed he wasn't Mr. Darcy.

Then the food came with baskets of fish tacos, fish and chips, one salad, drafts of beer, and another pitcher of that slushy drink. As our small group ate dinner, I learned several interesting facts from the local deadbeats and rule breakers. No one liked Mrs. Bennet. She was known far and wide as the neighborhood tyrant, and Caroline only socialized with Gail out of paranoia. Caroline's husband refused to walk their dog because of Gail and never took their dog to the park when Gail was there. Gail called animal control at least once every week with a new complaint about someone, for any little infraction, no one was spared. Grace was also convinced that Gail drugged the dogs, her own white fluff dog and others. Grace *knew* there was something in the doggie treats Mrs. Bennet doled out in the park.

"Seriously," Grace's dark eyes became sharp slits to match her sharp chin, she was a striking beauty. God had given her creamy skin and drew distinct features on that colorless cream with a soft dark charcoal grey pencil to give her a smoky look. "Have you noticed? She feeds those treats to excited, rambunctious dogs to calm them down. Mollie always becomes droopy and lethargic about fifteen minutes after one of those treats."

"Maybe you can steal one of the treats and have it analyzed," George smirked.

Grace glared at him. "She drugged Mollie, I'm sure of it. You don't care because you like it when she gives those treats to Bingo."

"Bengogh. His name is Bengogh. It's French. Like Van Gogh, but with a Ben."

They gossiped about the mysterious relationship between Mrs. Bennet and the smiley boy, Micah. Micah never refused an odd job from Gail, running errands, delivering notes, picking up shopping. Micah also walked dogs for her, Snowball and other dogs. He often did strange favors for people at Mrs. Bennet's bidding. I recalled how he ran in to scoop up Henry's poop without blinking an eye. No one knew exactly how that relationship began, but somehow, Mrs. Bennet acquired a very loyal errand boy.

"Another mystery," Grace said in a hushed voice. "Where are the minion's parents, and do they approve of Mrs. Bennet? I don't think anyone has ever met them. Doesn't anyone find that concerning besides myself?"

Caroline knew a little about Micah. He and the other boys lived in the large apartment complex kitty-corner from the dog park. Those boys could be seen all up and down Regency Park and on the walking paths, and at the Dollar Store near CSV. Very old school kids in that group, running wild and free all over the neighborhood.

"I think it's nice, giving him odd jobs. It can keep him out of trouble," Matt said softly.

George smirked, and everyone glanced at him, but he didn't say anything.

The evening passed pleasantly enough. The band played songs from the seventies and eighties, and lots of people danced, changing partners, but in a big group, laughing. We were a bit of a motley group. Older couples on one side, younger singles on the other. Caroline's husband arrived late and stayed for roughly five minutes before they left. Then, the Batten's left, followed by the Wilsons, and next Grace begged off. Grace worked early in the morning, she happened to be a teacher in the Sacramento City school district. They still had another two weeks of school before her summer break. She left money on the table, and the two fellows watched her leave. I noticed George taking care of the bill, accepting money from Matt, but ignoring my offered cash. I suddenly felt funny being left at the table with only Matt and George.

"I better go, too. I left Henry out back, and I have a workday tomorrow." I pulled out my phone to call an uber. "Thanks for inviting me. This was a lot of fun."

"Hey, don't call a car." Matt noticed the app. "I can drive you home."

I glanced at him and shot a look at George.

"It's okay, I'm taking George home, too. His bike is on my car. We can drop you at your house. We all live in Regency Park. I should have asked if you needed a ride, we could have picked you up."

George bobbed his head in agreement. He drained the last of the pitcher into his glass, then tossed it down his throat in one gulp.

Should I ride home with those two men? I barely knew them. Maybe I should have asked Grace for a ride, but I didn't know her well, either. I gazed at Matt with his messy, handsome hair and nice smile. It might be okay to accept a ride from someone who affected my limbic system in such an interesting way. It was only a short drive, and he seemed nice. I stared at Matt's bandaged hand.

"I'll agree if you promise to get a tetanus shot for your hand," I said.

Matt chuckled. "I think I'll live. It's only a little bite and getting a shot sounds like too much trouble. If it starts to look bad, I'll get a shot."

"It isn't too much trouble, and you don't want it to look bad. We give tetanus shots at the CSV, my treat. You probably should get that shot right away, tonight."

I insisted Matt drive us to the CSV first. I could log in all the information and personally administer the shot. The more I pondered that idea, the more it seemed like the responsible thing to do. That old dog, Old Major, did not look healthy. Anyone could see his haggard appearance and questionable health, and the bite went deep, it drew blood. If Matt waited for signs of an infection to manifest, he would have several bad days ahead. Better to be safe than sorry.

Okay, I admit, part of my overwhelming urge to give him a shot sprung from a secret desire to manhandle his arm. I might offer to clean his wound, too, and then I could get a feel of his Popeye forearm and get a close-up look at that hidden deltoid muscle, which, if the curve of his shirt didn't lie, should be massive. I'd also get to handle one extra bulky hand for a few minutes and that thought made me swallow guiltily. I realized I was very likely emerging from my social anxiety as a creepy stalker-type. Just look at how I spied on people and dogs from the comfort of my front window, and ogled the limbs on an unsuspecting wounded acquaintance.

CSV never closed, but the pharmacy window was only open between nine a.m. to nine p.m. The night cashier, Ernie Matthews, glanced up momentarily, but he went right back to his cell phone when he saw it was me. I often dropped in late at night. I'd been known to rearrange my desk, straighten the shelves, or catch up on the shredding late at night. It was a big part of my exciting life of anxiety and nerves and the lack of an impending test or exam to study for. If my mind wandered over something left undone or visualized something askew on my desktop, I couldn't fall asleep and took a late-night stroll that ended up at the CSV. It was on one of those late-night runs that I bought three paperback books off the self, *The Easy Macrobiotic Diet*, *Simple Trails of Northern California*, and that super thick romance novel, *Sins of the Duke*.

Matt and George followed me to the back pharmacy, and I invited them into my little office. I used my jumble of keys to work my way into the main storage area to gather shot materials. That meant unlocking the main glass doors, unlocking the grey metal cabinet, the small refrigerator, and retrieving one small vial of vaccine. I paused to log everything onto the written pad then locked things up as I backtracked to my office. I could see Matt and George watching me through the thick glass window and I grabbed the office first aid kit.

"Shot first," I announced when I slipped into the office.

George shot up. "I'm going to browse around." He moved toward the main store and I watched him pause at the glass door to the medicines. *Did he just test it to see if it was locked?* He glanced back and shrugged.

"Sorry about the backlog," I said, knowing full well we were fully stocked. "Maybe I can recheck the system and see if anything has shown up." Like digital confirmation from your doctor, I didn't add.

"Oh no, no, no, no problem," George said quickly. "I took care of it. No need to check anything." He left rather quickly to browse.

Matt pushed his sleeve up to expose one well-sculpted arm. His golden eyes were expectant, but a little worried. I gave him a nice smile and rubbed his rounded deltoid with a little cotton puff soaked with alcohol. Good grief, his upper arm muscles were just as defined as his forearms. Each large mass was etched distinctly into smooth tanned skin, tricep, bicep, deltoid. As I brought the needle into position, his eyelids squeezed tightly shut, wary of the shot. He was too cute! I pushed the needle into his arm, and a small tendril of his long hair fell out from behind his ear. I stopped myself from putting it back in place, but that just drew my eyes to his very hypnotic ear. It was all curves and mounds with large lobes, but swept back, perfect for keeping his wavy hair from his face. Never in my life had I noticed an ear before, but something inside of me imagined nibbling on that one. What harm would it do? Didn't he very recently get a tetanus shot for bites? Luckily, I had a little self-control when it came to men. Instead of biting his ear, I slapped a band-aide on the injection site.

Matt opened his eyes, relieved it was over, and he covered his nice deltoid and began to stand. But I reached over and held down his arm near the elbow. Warm, rock hard, and electrifying. I snatched my hand back at the minor shock, and when our eyes met, I could see he felt it, too. Static electricity? He licked his lips, *how completely erotic.* My pulse raced.

"Don't move yet," I said in a soft voice. "I'm cleaning your wound, too. I have topical antibiotic prophylaxis right here, and I'll bet you only rinsed it with a little water. Animal bites should never be taken lightly."

"Okay." His voice came out soft as he surrendered his arm for more of my ogling. He kept his eyes on my face, and I felt excited. Uncomfortable. Pretty. Most of the men I usually associated with were thin, pale, small, nerdy, and socially stiff, like me. Matt was the exact opposite of them, a bronze warrior. He was tall, muscular, attractive, and he felt exciting and spontaneous, sensual, *exactly like the duke in that scandalous novel,* handsome and maybe a little dangerous.

I opened his awful excuse for a bandage and concluded that he probably didn't even wash the wound with water. With a handful of alcohol-soaked cotton swabs, I cleaned up the dried blood recalling, *Maggie also cleaned the duke's wounds! That's when he first noticed her!* I rubbed the prophylaxis cream into every mark on his hand. Three round red dots marked the large mound of his palm and another at the base of his thumb. The skin around them appeared red and raw already, not a good sign. The flip side of his hand appeared a little bruised. His hands were twice the size of mine, and his skin felt rough, tough, and he had calloused fingertips. *Just like that duke, he had sinful hands!* I looked back at his eyes and felt the nerves along my skin tingle at the way he was gazing at me.

"You might want to see your doctor. To be sure nothing's broken."

"Nothing's broken," he said softly. "So, is he your boyfriend, Josh? Is it serious? You're taking care of his dog, right? But you haven't known him very long? Is he just a friend then? Am I out of line for asking this? I just..." He looked down at his hand. "Thank you for taking care of me here. You're very nice. Very nice and sweet. I'm just asking because it would be a shame if it's serious between you and Josh."

Was Josh my boyfriend? I didn't know. We went out on two official dates. He had come over to my house five times, with Henry, and we made-out on my couch every one of those times. It was very pleasant and very nice, and I even imagined it would get better. But not once did my heart go out of whack as it did at the sight of Matt's hands. Not once did I feel an urge to nibble on any part of Josh. Not once did his eyes make me melt inside like a puddle of warm, sweet chocolate. But I was taking care of his dog, right? Did that make him my boyfriend? Good grief, that dog Henry really knew how to stick his nose into my business!

"Oh, no," I said softly. "It's not serious."

Matt flashed the smallest hint of a smile as he pulled his treasured, wounded arm back into safety. Who knew what he was thinking? At least he didn't seem upset. I straightened up my small office and locked all the doors. We found George in the beauty section checking out the nail polish, then left. Matt and George dropped me off and waited until I went inside, then they drove off toward Regency Park Elementary School. I immediately let Henry into the house and gazed at him sternly.

"No sleeping in my bed tonight," I told him.

Henry just blinked with his sad doggy eyes. Was he upset about being left out back? Henry happened to be a hard dog to read. I patted his head and went off to bed. For the first time in my new house, I shut the bedroom door to sleep. I could do without the heavy breathing and drool on my bedsheets.

# Day Three

## with Henry

A sliver of golden sunlight filtered in between the curtains to wake me. I felt very light-hearted and happy. It was my day to pull the short shift, so I could laze a bit longer in bed. I glanced at Henry, who was back in bed with me, and noticed something in his mouth. What was it? Light blue, white, and stringy. Was that part of the area rug from the front room? My favorite small rug which was the perfect size and thickness for my daily yoga stretches? The one souvenir from India that I splurged on? I sat up in bed and stared at Henry.

"How did you get in here? I closed that door!"

Henry just stared at me and dropped the strands of cloth from his mouth. It tumbled out as a wet, slobbery, striped mess. Definitely strands from that rug.

"They tell me you peed on purpose, and it wasn't an accident," I accused Henry. "That you were marking your territory. Here's some news for you, buster. This house is *my* territory. You are a guest in *my* house! Please try to remember that."

Henry's tail thumped on the bed in a very endearing way, not concerned in the least with my raised voice. Henry certainly loved direct eye contact. I couldn't help the smile that cracked my lips at his goofy hanging tongue.

Sweet and nice. *Beautiful and sexy.* Did the same guy utter both those descriptions? Could Matt describe me in such different ways on the very same day? And had Matt noticed my teardrop lepidolite stone? I felt a little disappointed because it was much easier to imagine George throwing out words like *beautiful and sexy* to the hostess at the bar. He was flirtatious, and *sexy* was a flirtatious thing to say. *Deadbeats and rule-breakers.* Was Matt a deadbeat? Did he have a job or any prospects? His car happened to be an old Honda with a bleached-out hood, very messy on the inside. I shouldn't be so judgmental, but I wondered if he had a job.

Henry inched closer and looked at me from under his hooded brows. I couldn't help myself and massaged his head. His deep, golden-brown fur felt extremely soft under my hands.

"I like golden brown," I said to Henry. "It's a very pretty color."

But nobody liked golden brown so much they'd wanted it sprinkled all over their bedsheets. Henry had shed little bits of hair everywhere. Gross! I shooed him off the covers and set out to change all the linen. When I finally stepped into the living room, I saw the damage. Not only was my treasured area rug chewed at the edges, but the sofa was also damaged. Stuffing and threads spilled out of a large hole on the right edge of a curved arm. I glared at Henry as he calmly took his spot on the now tattered area rug. He plopped down and turned those melancholy eyes on me.

"Oh, Henry! When did you do this?" I asked the dog. "Did you have a late-night party?"

Henry yawned. He certainly had a late-night chewing party.

"Do not give me that innocent face!" Ugh! I stomped into the kitchen, found my phone. I punched in Josh's number. It went straight to voice mail. One text from Josh blinked in my notifications, a text with one line and a bunch of emojis.

*Hey babe, I'm sure you and Henry are doing fine, just sending my love,* followed by three hearts. That text came at two in the morning. Okay, I get it, Japan is on the opposite side of the globe.

One glance at the back yard, and I got another surprise. Large clumps of dog droppings lay in the grass, off the patio. *Gross!* And my mini potted olive tree, my only keepsake from home, was potted no more. *Murderer!* I rushed onto the patio to rescue the tree. Good grief, he chewed on the roots and limbs. That poor tree! And where did all the soil go? I glanced around and spotted the ceramic pot, broken in three. From inside the house, Henry stood at the sliding glass door bonking his nose at me.

"Oh, Henry!" I yelled. "Henry, why?" I felt close to tears.

Henry pushed his nose through the door and inched it open. He wandered onto the patio, and his melancholy face made him look as sad as I felt. But he didn't fool me. He was a monster. He was quietly torturing me and acting all innocent and clueless with those puppy dog eyes of his. I was going to leave him outside, as Matt suggested. It would be hot outside and Mrs. Bennet claimed it was dog abuse, but I was going to leave him outside! Good grief, I was actually crying, tears trickled down my cheeks. I felt Henry bonking me with his nose, and my eyes glanced at him, ready to send him another piercing glare. But he stood there, forlorn hooded eyes staring at me, *so sorry*, and in his mouth, he extended a small olive branch.

I did some research. How much would it cost to keep Henry in a kennel until Josh returned? Fifty-nine dollars a night was the short answer. That would pay for keeping him in a cage, all alone, fed twice a day, and let out of the cage once a day for fifteen minutes. More time out would cost more money.

Fees for all-day play and the cage at night bordered on nice hotel rates, and I might as well reserve him a room at the Hilton Express. If I opted for interactive play, it would be a slightly higher fee. Many dogs enjoyed a wash with water play, to relieve the stress of separation, for an extra little fee. Then, there was outside play, just a few dollars a day more. And the outside/inside combo play, another little fee. Or the outside/inside/water play combo, there was a discount. Adding in a special training or a socialization session was highly recommended. Really, a humane person wouldn't settle for anything less than the deluxe triple combo care package, with sudsy bath and socialization. It came with a bonus free dog bandana thrown in. It was especially recommended because I was hoping to board my dog for over a week.

The worst part. What would I say to my new friends, the dog park gang?

Another thing I researched: Gail Bennet was not in the system at CSV, Jane Bennet was. And Jane Bennet returned for another med-run order at the pharmacy. Doctor King rushed to the counter, chatting and helping the old lady with her order. They chuckled together like old friends. Gail kept her eyes on Doctor King and didn't notice me at all. She kept wiping her nose and coughing. Six large bottles of pills lay between them. I looked them up.

*Vicodin, Trazodone, Xanax, Percocet, Hydrocodone, Erythropoietin.* Jane Bennet was fetching medicine for people at the old folks' home again. John Seward, Justine Moritz, and Lucy Westenra needed help, and "Jane Bennet" volunteered her time. Everything looked ship-shape in the system. I spied Mrs. Bennet giggling with Doctor King between her nose wipes. Her eyes flashed up to me, and she momentarily appeared shocked to find me staring at her. She recovered, smiled, and waved. Doctor King glanced over his shoulder at me. Then, he finished up with Mrs. Bennet, and she disappeared down the aisle. She had a powerful walk for an older woman.

After a moment, Doctor King stuck his head in the door.

"I noticed you gave an after-hours injection last night."

"Someone was bitten by a dog," I nodded. "I happened to be around."

"As long as we don't make it a habit. No one wants to be on call around here. But it's a good thing you did it," he said. "Mrs. Bennet relayed the facts on that dog incident. They're suspicious about that dog and are checking for rabies, so I'm going to double-check our supply here. She said they put the dog down late last night to get to the bottom of it. She thinks she picked up a virus at the shelter, and I assured her that rabies is not an airborne virus."

He glanced around my small office. Doctor King must be close to sixty-five or seventy years old, or older. His hair was snow white, and his skin was spotted and wrinkled. He walked around the office ho-humming constantly throughout the day, singing under his breath. I think the tune was "Staying Alive" by the Bee Gees.

"You look very lovely today, Doctor Fitzgerald. I believe you've gotten more color from the sun. Mrs. Bennet says she met you at the dog park. Did you get a dog?"

"I'm dog-sitting," I told him. "I live directly across the street from the dog park."

"It sounds like fun." He chuckled and went off to help another customer.

The proper time to ask the doctor about Mrs. Bennet's name, or if he's seen her identification card, or how a fake name could be in the system never presented itself. But he seemed to know Mrs. Bennet well, everyone in CSV seemed to know her pretty well. The name must be a little joke between them. I wondered if anyone else from the dog park was aware Old Major had been put down. I wondered if he had rabies. He certainly didn't appear rabid, he just looked old.

As I walked the path along the levy, carrying a large plastic pot, a fast cyclist sped by. Then, he came to a stop and circled around. Bright blue skin-tight shorts and a green and yellow form-fitting shirt moved my way. George wore a dark safety helmet, and his red hair stuck out the top openings. His sunglasses were barely tinted, and they curved around his face. I knew nothing about cycling, but he certainly looked impressive. He inched toward me and came round to cycle at walking speed alongside me. How did he not fall over going so slow?

"Well, hello Doctor Sarah." He grinned. "Is this the route you walk to and from work?"

"It seems to be the shortest line between the two points." I nodded. "Is this part of your training route?"

"Oh, no," he said. "I'm heading onto Elkhorn, then I'll ride the levee roads and end up out past those rice fields. I'm going to try to get another thirty or forty miles today. Training, you know. It's a full-time job."

"Thirty or forty miles, wow." I couldn't imagine riding even two miles.

"I should clock in more than that, but there's only so many hours in the day. Work hours are always interfering with my training schedule."

"I can barely find time for my yoga anymore," I confessed. What I really meant was I could barely find *space* for my yoga anymore. It seems an overlarge drooling monster has claimed my yoga spot as his own.

"Someday, hopefully, I'll be able to train without constraint. If I rank high enough, I may land a corporate sponsor. But I need to clock in well. I keep telling folks I'll need a strong woman to be my cheerleader and man-the-ship when that happens. Someone who can take care of herself and doesn't need me meddling in with her ambitions. Someone who appreciates an athlete. I'd make a great house husband, I'm not afraid of being a kept man. I'm a feminist! The world is changing, don't you think?"

I wasn't exactly sure of the response he expected. It felt a little weird with him on his bike, riding at walking speed. I looked down at his shoes and realized they were connected to his pedals. George was still grinning at me. He looked in great shape, although his back appeared a bit hunched. The hunch was more pronounced when he was on the bike.

"I'm pretty progressive, don't you think?" he asked.

"Yes, very progressive." I agreed, but I had to look away when I said it.

His bike wobbled next to me. "Well, I'm going to press on. I've got at least thirty miles, minimum. Maybe I'll see you at the park later. I usually take Bengogh around five."

"Yes, maybe I'll see you there," I agreed.

To my relief, he sped off. Good grief, had he been flirting with me? I had no idea. Did he think I wanted a feminist man who wanted to ride a bike all day? Maybe he was making small talk. In regards to his spandex riding outfit, Mrs. Bennet was not off base when she questioned his choice to wear such revealing material.

As I turned the corner, I noticed something on my doorstep. It appeared to be a dustpan and small rake. A note was taped to the panhandle. I unfolded the note.

*For scooping up the dog poop. Keep it out of dog reach. Signed, M*

M! From Matt! How genius! A pooper scooper! I dreaded picking up those droppings in the backyard, but I did not want to leave them either. I hoped to run into Mrs. Bennet's young friend and discuss a little side job, but with this ingenious pooper scooper contraption, that wouldn't be necessary. I clamored into the house and out to the backyard with my new treasure. Henry was right where I left him, but clearly, he didn't stay there. The far corner of the lawn was no longer a green blanket. It was now a large dirt pile. I rolled my eyes at Henry and turned to the olive tree on the inside of the kitchen glass door, roots bagged and waiting to be replanted. I made a plan. Replant my mini olive tree, dispose of the yard poop, practice some yoga while baking, then take Henry to the dog park with cookies and a thank you.

Caroline and Grace chatted happily in Mrs. Bennet's spot, laughing loudly. Caroline gleefully waved me over as soon as I stepped into the gate. Henry strolled off to his favorite shady spot with his big nose sniffing around as he went. At the other end of the dog run, Matt and another man threw balls for the dogs. Matt raised his hand and waved, and I waved back rather enthusiastically, eliciting a chuckle out of

Grace and Caroline. I reeled it in a bit and offered each of them a chocolate chip cookie with walnuts.

"He left a pooper scooper on my porch," I said, trying to explain my enthusiasm.

"That sounds like true love," Grace teased and we all laughed.

Matt jogged up in a nice shirt and clean shorts. His hand was still wrapped in my bandage, and I was certain he hadn't cleaned it again. I offered him a cookie, and he happily took one. His amused gaze locked onto mine as he sat next to me. I'd never had such an attractive, physically fit man appear interested in me before. Wavy brown hair tumbled over his tanned face and a strong square jaw framed a nice smile. He could be a movie star with all those good features.

"How'd Henry do today? Has he been up to more mischief?" he asked.

The mention of that dog brought me back down a notch and I imagined my face showed it. Whatever my expression, all three of them giggled at my response. I didn't want to think about that dog. I was more concerned with Matt's hand.

"You need to keep your hand clean and put more antibiotics on it. I've got a tube of antibiotic prophylaxis in my house. I'd be willing to fix you up later, after Henry gets his hour in. You shouldn't let it go this long between cleanings, especially since it looked a little red and raw last night. Did you happen to inspect it again?"

Matt's eyes widened into an expression that said, *nope.*

"She's right. But why wait an hour?" Grace slowly shoved me off the bench. "Henry will be okay. He's just chilling in the shade. And Lola's Labs won't care a bit, I'm happy to watch them. I'm not going anywhere for a while, so why don't you two get lost over there and fix up that hand?"

What was Grace doing? Attempting to turn me into a rule breaker?

"Oh, no. That's one of the rules, right? *Never leave your dog unattended.* I wouldn't dare risk Mrs. Bennet showing up and discovering Henry was left alone again."

Caroline and Grace laughed, each glancing between Matt and me. Clearly, they could see my complete attraction to Matt Diller and thought they were doing me favor. Caroline leaned forward.

"Mrs. Bennet is not coming to the park today. Micah passed by a little while ago with Snowball in that ridiculous dog pram and said Gail was under the weather. If you're going to break any rules, this is the day to do it. Nobody here is going to tattle to Gail Bennet about anything. It's terrible the way that woman harasses people. I wish she would find another dog park to menace. It's so much more relaxing without her around, don't you agree?"

"Ding dong, the witch is gone! If we're lucky, whatever she caught will turn out to be a house falling on her head," Grace added with a chuckle. "No, I'm kidding. But having a Gail Bennet break sure is divine. Go on and clean up that man's wound. Matt is never going to clean it himself. Take advantage of today, no one cares if you leave Henry, and no one cares about Mrs. Bennet's rules. You're across the street for crying out loud, it's no big deal if you pop away for a few minutes to administer *first aid* to a friend. Just leave a couple of those cookies with us."

Matt followed me to my door. Sometime earlier that day, he had dropped that beautiful present on my doorstep. Had he hoped I was home? Gotten upset that he missed me? I invited him into my house and noticed his eyes shoot all around. I was usually a neat freak with everything clean and in its place, no dust, no clutter, no mess. The bookcase showcased a visual display of my favorite titles, all chemical textbooks and favorite figurines arranged in a geometrically pleasing pattern. I was glad I hid that one paperback book in my back bedroom. There was nothing I could do about the chewed-up area rug and damaged sofa. Matt took the entire room in as I pointed out the photo of my parents. Then, we passed into the kitchen where my newly potted mini olive tree sat perched on the small table. As I retrieved my first aid kit, Matt meandered toward the sliding glass door and surveyed the yard.

"Henry did all that?" He pointed to the torn-up lawn. "And the rug and the sofa?"

I nodded. "I don't know what I'm doing wrong." I motioned for him to sit down at the table and gingerly unwound the bandage I placed the night before. "I think I'm being nice. Henry seems so docile and quiet when we're together, but then I come home from work and discover my olive tree is destroyed, the grass is dug up. Last night, we sat quietly for hours as I patted him on the head while watching TV. But he must have needed more attention because he decided to chew up that rug and the couch while I was sleeping."

Matt's bite wound did not look worse, but it did not look better, either. The round marks were still surrounded by a slight pink, and I rubbed the cream onto his skin worried about that redness. His hand felt strong and rough, with long fingers and large knuckles. I let my eyes travel up his wrists to the radial muscles of his forearm before I rewrapped his hand. My heart was pounding. My goodness, I was becoming an absolute lech! I gave him back his hand as soon as I finished.

But Matt didn't let me get away. He caught my hand in his and pulled it toward him. He covered it with his good hand, and I felt a distinct trail of warmth snake through my veins as his hands embraced mine. I felt the beginnings of a flush creep over my face. Never had someone affected me like this. Literal shivers tingled over the skin he caressed.

"You aren't doing anything wrong," he said. "And you are nice. Very nice. Henry is acting out because his owner left him. It's not you, and it's not Henry. *It's Josh.* He should not have left his dog with someone who isn't used to having a pet. You should leave Henry outside, all the time. He'll be okay for a few days, until Josh gets back. He might tear up your yard, but at least he won't tear up your furniture. He's a big dog and can survive being outside, it won't kill him. You have plenty of shade back there." He gazed at me with his golden-brown eyes. "Thank you for taking care of this bite wound. You're pretty nice to me."

"No problem," I said. "And I wanted to thank you, for the scooper thing."

"The scooper thing?" He chuckled.

He obviously did not leave the small rake and scooper pan on my doorstep. Who did? I just shook my head at his confused eyes.

"What do you think about this idea?" he asked. "Maybe we can... What do you think about going somewhere sometime? With me, I mean."

"That might be nice."

"Maybe we can go out for ice cream. There's a Cold Stone over in the Park Place Plaza. Or we can go see live music again, but maybe leave the others out of it. There's a barn out in Davis, a brewery that hosts live music sometimes. It's a hops farm. Or maybe we can take the dogs out on a hike."

"Any of that sounds nice," I said.

"Good." He kissed my hand softly, before shyly releasing it.

That caused me to wonder if he might try kissing me on the lips. *Please, Matt, try kissing my lips.* I sent him the mental message, then focused on straightening up my medical supplies, to keep from staring at his mouth, or face, or insanely muscular arms. What was this? I barely knew this man, and he was the exact opposite of everything I imagined in a perfect partner. He didn't appear to have a regular job, he was usually very messy, he drove a beat-up old car with oxidized paint on the hood, didn't own a home of his own, and was very careless about infection...But his forearms were like Popeye the Sailor Man and I had an olive tree. Wasn't that a cosmic sign?

We slowly stood and moved back into the living room to glanced through the dog park viewing window. Henry hadn't moved an inch from his shady spot, and Grace and Caroline were still perched on the bench in an animated conversation. George now stood next to them, laughing with them. He wore his cycling attire, sans the helmet. It was hard to determine if anyone could see into my window, but now and then, one of them glanced toward my house. Matt stared intently out at the park.

"Joe still hasn't shown up. Maybe the shelter didn't release Old Major yet. I hope they let that old dog out soon. I feel terrible about what happened. I should have pulled my hand away sooner. I know old Joe is going to worry about this bite. Old Major is about the only company Joe has, and it wasn't the dog's fault."

*Matt didn't know…* Old Major would never be let out of the shelter! That meant no one in the dog park was aware about Old Major. Mrs. Bennet clearly said the dog had been put down. That's what she told Doctor King. And they were testing him for rabies. Didn't that require a brain sample? That test shouldn't take long, so they might even have the test results by now. Or perhaps they hadn't removed the test sample yet. Maybe the dog was sent to an out of shelter vet for the extraction of dura mater. Thank goodness I insisted on giving Matt that shot and the antibiotic cream. I just wish he had cleaned his wound properly right away. If the test came back positive, he'll need to have another vaccination, a series of them.

"What's wrong?" Matt must have seen my worried eyes.

"Something I heard at the pharmacy. Mrs. Bennet told Doctor King that Old Major was...he was...they put him..."

"They put him down!" Matt stiffened.

We rushed out of the house and back to the dog park. Caroline and Grace appeared confused at our reentrance. Maybe they expected us to return in a different state, with different expressions, in a different mood. But nothing killed a romantic moment like news of an animal being put down at a shelter. Everyone straightened up at our return, realizing something very wrong had occurred. I found myself relaying the gossip to all of them.

"That wicked witch! She probably demanded they put Old Major down. Insisted on it!" Grace sputtered. "Why the hell does she stick her fat nose in everywhere? Poor old Joe!"

Caroline appeared stricken.

"He didn't have rabies," George added softly. "He clearly did not have rabies."

Matt ran his hand over his head. "Someone should check on Joe. I'm not sure where he lives, does anyone know where he lives?"

Nobody knew.

"He does tend to head in the direction of the foot park, you know, past the CSV with all the soccer fields," Caroline said softly. "I've seen him walking over there. I'll bet Bob knows."

"I'm going to find out," Matt said. "And I'm going to check on him." He whistled loudly, and his two Labradors, chocolate Bluebell and black Stella, stopped moving on the other end of the park and turned to him. Matt called them over, then frowned back at us as he rushed to the gate. "I'm going to head home and try to check up on Joe. I'll call Bob, and I'll call the shelter and find out exactly what happened out there." And then Matt and the Labs were gone.

"Someone should give that woman a dose of her own medicine." Grace narrowed her eyes. "She is so incredibly disgusting with her bullying. I can't believe Old Major is actually gone."

Caroline agreed. Then, she called her yellow Lab and left, very upset.

George took her place on the bench next to Grace, and the three of us sat quietly for several minutes before George suddenly stood and jogged across the park. He delivered the sad news to the men throwing balls for the dogs. I glanced at Henry, and Henry glanced back. He stood up and slowly meandered toward me. *How did he know I wanted to go?*

"Just so you know," Grace whispered to me as I stood to retrieve Henry, "I have never seen Matt wear a button-down shirt before, ever. And today, and yesterday, you could say he was dressed up. I think it has something to do with you. Please be nice to Matt, he's my best friend's brother, and I think he's been through a lot."

Good grief, what had he been through?

Matt advised me to keep Henry outside, but by ten at night, a light sprinkle began to fall and the low rumble of thunder rolled overhead. The towering clouds over the mountains must have successfully slipped into the valley. I couldn't leave Henry out in the rain during a thunderstorm, but perhaps I could house him in the hall bathroom for the night. There was nothing he could chew up in there. I felt a bit mean, because it was a tiny room, but it was bigger than the forty-eight-inch crate that cost fifty dollars a night at the doggie hotel. My hall bathroom could be considered luxury accommodations compared to a forty-eight-inch crate.

Henry gazed up at me calmly, and it was hard to decipher if he felt sad to be banned to the bathroom or happy to be out of the rain. Henry was unreadable. He lay on the shaggy toilet seat rug I was destined to replace in the near future. I considered trying to wrestle it out from under him, but his body practically hid the entire small rug, and those dejected eyes didn't fool me: He was not letting that little bit of shag go.

"Fine," I surrendered to Henry. "But I wish you'd spare that rug tonight. If you meant it at all with the olive branch earlier, you won't chew up my rug. Just remember who's keeping you from a wet night outside."

I closed the door firmly and went off to bed.

# Day Four

## with Henry

On days off, I'd developed a fondness for sleeping in. Nothing pleased me more than lingering deep below the covers and curling cozily on my king-sized bed, while clinging to the last tendrils of a dream swirling in the cavities of my mind. I hardly ever remembered my dreams, but I was certain this one revolved around golden brown eyes and smooth tan-colored skin standing under a waterfall with a little heavy breathing that could be passion but somehow sounded slightly off. My thick curtains completely blocked out the light, so it wasn't morning sunshine that woke me up. It was the pungent aroma. And the heavy breathing. And the waterfall. And the wet tongue on my wrist. *No!* I sat up in bed and stared down at him, the nemesis of my good mornings. My pleasant dream had warped into a nightmare.

"How did you escape from the bathroom?" I asked, then realized with a sinking, plummeting heart that Henry was *completely soaking wet!* Like he had taken a long bath and decided to drip dry on my king-sized comforter. His tail thumped happily at our eye contact. Did I still hear the echo of a waterfall? *Oh no!* I jumped out of bed and raced to the hall bathroom.

"Oh, Henry!"

The bath was running, plus the shower and the sink, and liquid covered the entire room from floor to ceiling. The lovely rose-shaped soaps I set out for guests, should they ever visit, were chewed into small crumbles and scattered all around in a sudsy mess. The cabinet door under the sink stood wide open with the extra toiletries scattered and spread out. Soaking toilet paper was plastered to the toilet, on the sink, in the bath, against the wall. The towel rack lay on the ground, and someone, I refused to name names, had crushed it so that the metal was slightly bent into a curve. I turned off every spigot and faced around gingerly to get a look at the door. That same unnamed someone had ripped the inside knob right off the door and the small shag toilet rug was mysteriously missing...or was it?

Henry hesitantly showed himself right outside the door. He glanced around the bathroom with a perplexed expression under his hooded brow, as if he wondered, who could do such a terrible, horrible thing. He clutched the toilet rug in his jaws.

*Look*, he seemed to say. *I saved it from being part of that wet watery mess, as you wished. It's perfectly fine.* And it was. Not a single shag was out of place. He set the small shag bathroom rug on the floor right outside the door as his tail thumped happily. His eyes watched me, expectantly. He sat at attention like a nice proper dog, happy to please his owner, and I couldn't help melting at those eyes of his, a sucker for a pretty face. I let my heavy, angry breathing settle down. Maybe, I reasoned, Henry had been hungry and thirsty. Maybe, I concluded, he felt trapped too long in that locked-up room. After all, I did sleep far into the morning. It was already half-past nine.

"Next time," I said softly, looking at the small perfect toilet rug, "I'll be more specific."

After mopping up the bathroom and settling down with Special K with dried strawberries, the phone rang. Matt! He apologized for "bugging out so fast the day before." He hoped to take me out to ice cream and thought it'd be nice to walk the dogs to the Cold Stone Creamery. He remembered I mentioned it was my day off. He could help me spend some time with Henry and maybe get an idea of the dynamics at play between us. He didn't claim to be a dog expert, but maybe Henry needed to be taken on a long walk somewhere new. A hound dog must desire new scents now and again. Plus, Matt had a burning desire to buy me an ice cream cone and hoped I'd accompany him when he dropped in on Joe. He asked if Henry behaved the previous night.

"A disaster. My guest bathroom is still drying out," I reported softly.

"You didn't leave him outside?"

"It was raining, with thunder. And lightning," I explained. There was a long pause.

"I have an igloo."

Pardon me? What did he just say?

"Did you just say that you have an *igloo*?"

"Yes," he said. "I have an igloo in the garage."

Oh my goodness, was it the rabies talking? Was he burning up? Is that why he had a burning desire for ice cream and was thinking about igloos? Was he imagining the arctic? Cold on the outside, hot on the inside?

"Seriously," he continued. "Lola won't mind. Stella and Bluebell don't use it. It's just sitting in a heap in the garage. I can bring it over, and Henry will have shelter from the elements. You can borrow it until Josh returns for his dog, no problem. I'm sorry I can't take Henry over here, but Lola would kill me. She's got strict house rules, and I don't think Henry is ready for strict house rules. If this was my own place..."

"Oh, you mean a dog house!" I started chuckling. "I'm so silly. And thank you for wanting to take Henry off my hands, but I wouldn't dream of unloading him on you. He's a sneaky destructive monster. I sent Josh a message asking if someone else could take him, but I haven't heard back yet. In the meantime, I'd love to borrow the… igloo," I said. "And I'd love to go out for ice cream, too, with you."

Matt wore another button-down shirt and nice clean shorts. He shaved, clearly washed his hair and added that gel, and smelled extra nice. *He was dressed up!* I noticed he removed the bandage. The bite marks looked fine, no more redness, and his hand was healing nicely. After setting up the dog igloo on my back patio, we set out on a brisk walk toward the local plaza to find ice cream. All three of the dogs walked beside us on the trail and Matt made a comment about Henry heeling nicely, perfectly. Henry acted just like a well-trained dog. I learned a little about Matt on our walk to Cold Stone.

He was brave. He had been a firefighter up in Washington state and worked fires since his seventeenth birthday. He was tech-savvy. He now worked a freelance job that involved computer programming and website design. He was family-oriented. He came down to California to help his sister in her time of need. His older sister Lola, actually named Karlola, was in the air force and on a long deployment somewhere in the Persian Gulf, flying cargo planes from place to place. She was stationed at Beal Air Force Base and bought the house in Natomas because it was halfway between her military station and her ex-boyfriend's office in Dixon. She was due back in fifteen days and Matt needed to make a plan for when she returned, because she wanted to sell the house and move.

"She's at the end of her commitment and is lined up to fly for FedEx when she gets out. She wants a place closer to the hub in Oakland."

Matt and his sister grew up in a small town in Washington State. Their parents both passed away years ago, so he was an orphan, like me. Matt moved temporarily to Sacramento to help his sister with the dogs. Her flying schedule became much too busy, and the guy she adopted the Labs with bugged out after her first long mission. He couldn't handle a girlfriend who flew away all the time. At first, Lola searched for new homes for the Labs, but Matt offered to help. It was easy to do with his freelance computer work, and he loved the outdoor activities around Sacramento. He played guitar, hiked, and kayaked on the river. In the winter, the local mountains offered plenty of snowboard trails, and there were interesting microbreweries with original music to keep him happy. He confessed that he had never dated a college graduate before, let alone one with a higher degree. He wondered if pharmacy school was very challenging.

"A little," I said. Try, very intense and competitive with a heavy schedule and rotations, not unlike medical school. Sleepless, mind-numbing, and riddled with land mines to take out the weak of heart every step of the way. It was a wonder I survived. After years of isolation from normal people and conversations that mainly revolved around chemical texts, I was surprised I could still communicate in a regular way. And here I was, planning to do it all over again starting this winter.

The Park Place Plaza was a very busy shopping square on Truxel Road across from the local high school and new aquatics center. There was a Jack's Urban Eats, a burger place, sushi place, taco restaurant, and a pool supply store surrounding the Cold Stone Creamery. Across the parking lot, there were other retail stores, but that little ice cream shop was hands-down the most popular place on the corner. A small line spilled out the door. We took the dogs to a far table and Matt whipped out two collapsible bowls. He filled them with water, and we loosely hooked each leash to a table, then we got in line for ice cream.

A cup of Founder's Favorite and a waffle cone of Strawberry Surprise later, we relaxed at the table, sitting with our three very well-behaved canines. Matt probably believed I had made up the stories of Henry's bad behavior, because Henry proved to be a calm, cool, character in front of witnesses. I glanced at that hound dog. Did he realize his perfect behavior caused my gripes to appear like crazy hysteria?

"I got Joe's address from the shelter," Matt said. "He lives right down that street toward the elementary school and the foot park. They didn't want to give it out at first, but I told them I was the one Old Major bit, and I wanted to let Joe know there were no hard feelings."

"Did they say anything about the rabies test?"

"They didn't know, but said Joe may have been notified by now. They said Old Major was very old and in lots of pain. It was more of a mercy situation than the fear of rabies, so they expect a negative test. That woman, Gail Bennet, went down there and was pretty relentless. Jay, the guy I spoke to, said she broke Joe down until he finally gave consent for the rabies test. Mrs. Bennet claimed the father of the boy insisted, but I don't believe it for a minute. Nobody knows that man or the boy. Mrs. Bennet also claimed that I demanded the rabies test too, which is a big fuck— fat lie. Would you mind walking past Joe's house on the way back, it's just over there? We could stop and check on him. I want to clear the air. He's an old man, and I think that dog was his only friend."

"Sure," I said. "It's over there? Maybe we can bring him a pint of ice cream. Do you think it'll melt?"

Matt smiled beautifully. "That's a great idea."

We decided on a mix of strawberry and vanilla with chips of chocolate mixed in. Joe's weather-worn home fell one block down and two blocks over, a large one-story house with a weed-filled, raggedy-edged yard. In the drive, an old Ford truck with real steel bumpers sat at an angle. It had a flat tire and a cracked, taped-up rear window. All five of us, Matt, me, and the three dogs, stood waiting after Matt rang the bell. The house stayed quiet. We rang the bell again. Nothing. Then, Matt knocked hard just in case. The impact of his knocking got the door shaking, and very slowly, the door creaked ajar. Matt flashed me a look, then leaned toward the open crack. My anxiety kicked in and filled me with trepidation.

"Joe!" Matt called into the house. "Joe! Are you in there?"

A long eerie silence followed his call, and Matt helped the door open more. I took a step backward. Was that okay? Opening someone's door? *Rule breakers and deadbeats* echoed in my ear.

"Joe, it's me, Matt! From the dog park. Joe, are you in there?"

Matt pushed the door completely open and we got a clear view into the front room, and a small hall that led into darkness. The house was a mess with stained carpet, paper and mail stacked high on furniture, and the musty smell of unaired space wafted out. My heart began to beat faster, and I felt a warm flush crawl up my neck. I worried about our actions, was this considered breaking and entering? What if we got the wrong house?

"Matt..." I started softly.

He glanced back at me. "I don't like the feel of this. Something's not right." He walked right into the large quiet house. He boldly stepped deeper and deeper into that darkness. Were we violating Joe's privacy? I hung back with the dogs, unsure of what to do. Matt disappeared around a corner, then I heard him shout.

"Joe!"

I dropped the leashes.

"Joe, Joe! Help!"

I ran into the house.

"Sarah! Call 911! Sarah!"

I turned the corner to find Matt crouched over a man lying on the ground. *A dead man. A body. A lifeless hunk of flesh.* Matt checked for a pulse, he checked for breathing, his eyes searched for signs of life, stricken. He ran a hand through his long wavy hair.

"Call 911!"

But I was already punching the numbers into my phone. By the look in Matt's eye, I could see he didn't detect any signs of life. No pulse, no breathing, no heat, no nothing. By the look of Joe, he appeared quite stiff and definitely was not expecting us. My worst fear had manifested right in front of me, a cadaver. *Dead people scare me like you wouldn't believe.*

My mind flashed on the dead people I had seen. My mother in her coffin lying like a deflated version of the woman I loved, while my ten-year-old self became hysterical, refusing to believe the body had been my mother. The body in the coffin was a grotesque, badly fashioned copy of my mother, and I became anxious, wondering where they hid the real body and why. *Was she still alive?* For years, I suffered through dark dreams of searching for my mother and almost finding her, but she always lay just out of reach, hiding from me.

Then, much later, I found my father sitting stiff and stern in his swivel desk chair with his eyes blankly fixed in the direction of the tome on his desk. My heart pounded into a frenzy as I realized why he had not greeted me at the airport on my first visit back from college. He had been too busy reading and dying alone in his study when I stood abandoned at the airport, upset that he forgotten me again. Somehow, I never quite felt whole after that particular day, the day I became truly alone in the world.

Then, the cadaver lab popped into my head. Sixteen shrunken bodies under bright lights and shrouded by white blankets waiting to be coldly analyzed. I had fainted at the first glimpse of a stiff, lifeless arm uncovered by my amused lab partner. I stood up and left, and never went back to that lab again.

Matt had a hard time tilting the cadaver's head back, and I knew the time for resuscitation had come and gone. I shook my head at Matt. He knew it too, but didn't want to admit it. I turned and wandered back toward the front door becoming cross-eyed with inquietude. I spoke shakily to the emergency operator. When I stepped back into the sunshine, I noticed all three dogs sitting obediently, waiting. But that pint of ice cream was on the ground, torn open.

*Oh, Henry.* He was the only one with the evidence on his lips. We were both a mess.

Several people from the dog park gathered in my living room, leaving their dogs across the street to run amuck with very little supervision. Mrs. Bennet would have an aneurysm if she showed up. No one cared about the rules anymore. People crossed over to my house for the news about Joe and Old Major, and that information was being broadcasted live from my living room via Matt. The two dozen cookies I baked the day before came to good use, and I was happy to provide something besides crackers to my unexpected guests. I brewed coffee and tea and brought out the little bits of cheese I had left. George fetched wine and beer. He zipped to the CSV at some time during the neighborhood news conference and brought back those extra items, because folks wanted to hear the gossip over and over again, and Matt repeated everything many, many times.

"It must have been a heart attack." Matt shook his head, sitting on the sofa next to Grace and a man I never met. "Or maybe a stroke."

Steam seemed to vent from Grace's ears. She drank tea and glared at the wine George offered.

"He was heartbroken," someone said. "He couldn't live without his loyal companion."

"Jay at the shelter said *that bitch* insisted on a rabies test. She insisted! Said the man and boy with the bite insisted! Fuck that! Fuck, fuck, fuck! Do you think he died thinking I wanted that? I certainly never insisted on anything like that. Has anyone seen the boy or the dad? I feel like wringing her neck."

Matt was furious. This was not a pretty side of him, but he was in shock from finding a dead body. The body of a man I never spoke with but watched daily for about a month through my front window. Every day, Joe would sit on that bench and nod to people and dogs. Now, he would never nod again.

Folks kept glancing out my window at the dog park. Were they checking on their dogs, or were they waiting for someone to drop in? Maybe they were waiting for Gail to arrive.

"Joe would never agree to put Old Major to sleep." Caroline shook her head. "I know he wouldn't. But with Gail breathing down his neck, what could he do? He probably died of guilt or regret. Eric refuses to bring Rosie to the park because of her. He's afraid of what he might do if he sees Mrs. Bennet."

"Someone needs to teach that woman a lesson." Grace stared through the window. "Do you think she's heard about Joe yet? Do you think she realizes the results of her constant bullying? I bet she's avoiding the park today because she doesn't want to face us. She knows she's responsible. Look, there's her little minion."

The boy Micah appeared along the far side of the park with Snowball in a doggy pram. Mrs. Bennet must still be under the weather, or hiding. When he passed near my house, Micah told someone on the porch that Mrs. Bennet was busy planning her weekly tea.

When Bob entered the dog park with his wet black lab, Matt popped off the sofa. He wanted to speak with the older man and relay the afternoon events all over again. He drew a few of the other folks out of my living room in his sprint to the dog park. But it wasn't enough. I desperately needed all of my guests to leave. Would it be strange for me to hide in my bedroom for a while?

"Did you try CPR?" Grace asked softly.

I shook my head. "Rigor mortis had already set in."

"God, that must have been crazy scary to find him like that."

I nodded. It certainly was. I was still shaky and kept my hands pressed under my pits so no one would notice. Grace headed back to the park, taking the rest of my guests with her. I stepped outside because Matt stood staring at my house, waving.

"I've got to go," he called over. "I'm going to take the Labs home. Do you need a hand cleaning up? Bob and I are going to go to the shelter."

George stood right next to me on the porch. "I'll help her clean up!" he volunteered.

We stood on my porch and watched quietly as the dog park cleared out. Most everyone puttered away frowning. Joe and Old Major had been daily characters at that park and would be sorely missed. George followed me back inside and helped pick up mugs and disposable cups. He glanced at the hole in the sofa and then at Henry in the backyard. I saw him peek down the hall toward my bedroom after perusing the books on my shelves. Then, he was suddenly at the kitchen sink rinsing out the mugs with the hot water running fast. He stared at the coffee maker and creased his brow.

"Shall I rinse this out?" he asked.

"Don't bother. I'll do it later."

"Oh, hey, are you okay?" His nearly transparent, almost albino eyes were full of concern.

I was not sure why I puddled into an emotional mess. The day had just been so overwhelming. First the bathroom, then the ice cream date, then the dead man. Why did I fear the dead so much? Would I ever stop seeing flashes of my dead mother lying oddly in her coffin or my dead father stiff in his chair with wide-open empty eyes? The emotional roller coaster of that day was far too crazy for my repressed emotional stress, and the strain of holding in the stress was just overwhelming. My heart had been pounding at a ticked-up speed for hours, and I felt exhausted as that racing muscle finally slowed down. The crowd of people Matt invited into my sanctuary didn't help matters, either. I hadn't realized how wound up I felt until everyone left and my nerves began to relax from being wrung out all day. I felt a river of wet hot tears rolling down my cheeks that I absolutely could not control. How embarrassing, crying in front of George.

He took two steps across the kitchen and embraced me. At first, I was mortified. But the pressure of his arms was exactly what I needed to squeeze out the last remnants of tension. He held me tight and added more pressure when he heard me sigh. I felt the pent-up energy drain right out of me, puddling to the floor. After a very long hug, he let me go and stood back. I nodded at him.

"Thank you, I needed that."

"I did, too," he said. "Joe was a good guy."

Then, I had my house to myself, all to myself. Everyone had gone, and Henry was in the backyard. He had his own home now, an igloo. *Good luck tearing up that chunk of hard plastic*, I thought. Then, I felt slightly guilty for being so petty on such a sad day.

# Day Five

## with Henry

I didn't feel guilty for long. After a very restless night, I finally just lay with my eyes open staring at the ceiling. The tangled mix of guilt about Henry, sadness about Joe and Old Major, anger at Josh, and heated thoughts about Matt stirred my insides. The last thing I did before getting into bed was to text Josh and clarify that *he was not my boyfriend* and *he needed to have someone come and get Henry.* That whimpering sound outside was Henry. Around two o'clock in the morning, I heard a soft bonk, bonk, bonk and at first was terrified. I glanced at the sliding door that connected my master bedroom to the back porch and noticed the big black nose tapping the door. Henry's signal. He wanted to come in. *Fat chance.* Dogs with big black noses were supposed to sleep outside on the top of dog houses! I'd seen tons and tons of pictures attesting to that fact. How else would he meet a little yellow bird and get a BFF for life? Then, I saw the blinking message from Japan.

*Oh no! What did Henry do? I'm so sorry babe. I'll try to fix this.*

Josh never once verbally referred to me as babe in person, and now he had called me babe twice in text. His phone went straight to voicemail although I knew it must be broad daylight in Japan. I certainly hoped he meant to fix the *babysitting* situation and not the *he's not my boyfriend* part of the message. I needed things cleared up with Josh, so I could focus on Matt. I laid in bed thinking about Matt and Joe, and stewing about that big black nose outside.

When the first light of day streamed into the house, I rolled out of bed and stumbled to my kitchen to put on the kettle. One look out the back sliding glass door told me everything I needed to know. Henry completed hated my backyard. My entire small patch of grass was now a rough and tumble dirt pile, and the few bushes against the fence were no longer rooted in the ground. Just one small square of lawn on the near corner next to the patio remained. And on that sparse grass, a large pile of Henry offerings sat waiting for the scooper.

Henry himself lay half out of his new igloo, drooling, with an innocent expression on his long face, like he had tried to warn me about the midnight yard wreckers, but I completely ignored him. I stepped outside to feed him, pat his head, then went back inside. After yesterday, a little torn-up yard didn't seem like anything to cry about. I left the door open but the screen closed, so he wouldn't feel entirely shut out.

"See, Henry, we can see and hear each other. It's what is known as a compromise."

Morning yoga, here I come. I needed serenity. It was a tight and tense morning. I did double my basic stretches as I looked out the front window. The early dog crowd was active. Joe and Old Major had been part of the morning walkers, too. They always appeared as I left for work, and they were there in the evening when I got home. Joe's bench sat empty, and people glanced at it, arms across chests, heads bent toward each other shaking sadly. The gossip must be flying.

Mountain pose, cat pose, downward-facing dog, warrior, and finally, the dreaded tripod headstand with lotus legs, my daily challenge. I didn't want to do it. I procrastinated for five minutes until there was a sharp knock at my door. *I hoped that he would come!* Wished it in the wee hours when I couldn't sleep and ingested more of that CSV novel. I was worried about him, my ice cream buddy. Now he was my knight in shining armor, saving me from the blood-rushing headache an upside-down lotus could sometimes bring.

But I was sorely disappointed at who presented themselves on the other side of my front door. He carried two Starbucks cups and a paper bag of something yummy. He grinned in a mischievous way as he offered the coffee. He wore a vintage concert T-shirt and casual shorts, sunglasses on the top of his red head. He was dressed like a normal man and confidently gazed at me.

"I felt bad that we ate and drank all your food," he said.

"George Wickham," I nodded at him. "Good morning."

There was a slight flinch in his pale blue eyes, and I wondered if he sensed my disappointment. I immediately felt bad about that and accepted the coffee. I invited him to sit on the sofa and spy on the dog park with me. Everyone in the park avoided Joe's bench. George pulled out treats from his bag. Apple fritter, old-fashioned donut, banana walnut bread. I certainly wasn't going to do the tripod headstand and lotus legs with him sitting there, so I took part of the banana walnut bread.

"I have a confession to make," George said. He looked nervous.

*Please, no confession*, I silently begged. I hoped that tight hug the previous night had not gone to his head. I had been in shock. I had seen a dead man. I had no time to process anything before that hug. I admitted, I needed it, but I did not need any confessions from George Wickham. It would end badly, didn't he read the novel?

"My name isn't George Wickham," he said, "It's George Johnson."

"What?" This was not the confession I had feared, but it caused a sort of fear somewhere in the back of my mind anyway.

"I used the Wickham name at CSV because..." He looked all around the room. "Well, I thought it would be okay because Gail uses the Jane Bennet name, and I thought it was some sort of code you guys used. I should have known better."

I was absolutely confused.

"That prescription was only for me, I assure you. I'm not some drug dealer or anything. I need certain substances for training purposes, and it's very expensive going through the middle man. I was trying to cut out the middle man."

I suddenly stood up. George *Johnson* also stood up. Good grief, he had faked a prescription. Thank goodness we didn't fill it! I stared at him wondering who I was looking at. I could practically see the gears shifting into motion behind those transparent eyes of his. He creased his red brow slightly, indignant. He was a good foot taller than me, and I didn't know how I was going to get him out of my house. I would gladly do that tripod lotus flower instead of this!

"I think you should leave," I said.

He shook his head. "That's not fair. The pills are for my personal legitimate use, and believe it or not, my supply has always come from your stock room. And I know you guys weren't backlogged because *she* was able to pick them up without any problem, and now *she's* trying to milk me for attempting to skirt her. So don't act like it isn't something that can't be done. I'm just trying to cut out the middle man, it's expensive." His eyes softened. "And we're friends, right? We're friends. I'm being honest with you here."

I tried to walk to the door, but he grabbed me by both arms and held me in place.

"We had a moment last night." His voice was desperate. "Didn't we have a moment? I felt it. I know you felt it." Then, he bent down and kissed me.

There was nothing sweet about that kiss. It felt like an assault. My two hands slammed to his chest, and I shoved him off me with such force that he stumbled two steps backward. His pale eyes appeared completely stunned.

"Get out!"

"This isn't fair."

Loud barking mixed with low growls suddenly filled the entire room. Startled, we both faced the kitchen and saw Henry with his paws on the screen door. His eyes were no longer sad, they were angry. Then, his paws pushed that flimsy screen door right off the track, and he leapt into the room. George scrambled to the door and fumbled clumsily with the knob. He just escaped out the door as the growling, barking Henry reached me. Henry instantly went quiet and turned his melancholy blinking eyes on me. After a moment, he strolled over to claim my yoga spot again, ensuring there'd be no tripod lotus poses that day. I sunk to the floor next to him and stroked his wrinkled, silky fur, trying to calm my racing heart and uneven breathing. I didn't even care that he still had soil from the torn-up lawn on his paws.

"Oh, Henry." My voice wavered softly. "You are so surprising."

Matt came round later in the day, right after noon. He apologized for running off so suddenly, but he wanted to go to the shelter with Bob. Apparently, Gail had filed a complaint against Bob the previous day. Gail had filed three complaints at the shelter the previous day, actually. Caroline might not know it yet, but there was a complaint against her yellow Lab Gatsby for humping other dogs and also a complaint about Grace for leaving Mollie in the park while she went out jogging.

"Grace jogs on the outside of the fence! She doesn't even go anywhere." Matt stared at the misshapen screen door propped against the wall. He walked toward the glass door, surveying the yard. "Henry did all this?"

"It's fine." I looked over at Henry, still in my yoga spot, drooling on the chewed area rug "He had his reasons. I called a handyman to fix it. To fix everything."

Matt put his hands on top of his head as he stared at my torn-out lawn, and his T-shirt rode up high enough for me to get a glimpse of sun-browned skin on his back. But it wasn't smooth looking. My pulse picked up as I glimpsed the line of his spine as it passed down toward his rock-hard ass. I was definitely a lech. He turned back to me, and my eyes snapped back to his face.

"If you have a rake, I can smooth it out for you. It's a pretty small yard. It won't be a problem to sod it. Or, if you're patient, you can seed it. But I think you should wait until Henry is picked up to do any of that." He glanced at the lounging hound dog. "I can't believe that hound dog. It's no wonder Josh left him with you after only knowing you a few weeks. I bet no one he knows would take him."

We went out on the back patio and Matt found my rake leaning against the side of the house. He ignored my protests and went to work trying to smooth out the mess. I watched, ogling his flexing arms as he worked. I loved the way his overlong hair bent around his ears and spilled onto his neck, and now I felt like biting his neck instead of his ear. I was a lech and a vampire. I loved that he was taller than Josh, and George, and straighter. I wondered what terrible things he had been through. I wondered if he would take his shirt off and give me a better look at his back and chest. I wondered if I was totally terrible for objectifying him so blatantly.

"Are you good friends with George?" I asked.

"I guess so," he said. "We're dog park buddies. We hang out in the park and the occasional Swabbies meet up. He's very focused on his bike training. Not my sport. Grace says he hits on all the younger women. He can come on pretty strong. I think she made a mistake with him once, that's how she put it." His golden eyes suddenly fixed on me. "Did he hit on you?" He took three steps toward me and stopped.

Should I tell him? About the kiss, the hug, the false name, the drugs? I wasn't sure what to say or how to say it. But clearly, I didn't need to say anything. Matt's eyes had darkened as he moved slowly toward me.

"Are you okay? Did he cross a line? Say something stupid? He can be an asshole."

I shook my head, but he could see something may have happened.

He stayed about a foot away from me. He was the perfect height and gave off an earthy, sweet aroma. His golden eyes were friendly, and his smile was pleasant, and just below his shirt, I could feel the energy radiating off those bulging muscles. I could not remember the last time someone had affected me like Matt Diller. In fact, I didn't think anyone had ever affected me like Matt Diller...except maybe the duke in that erotic romance novel from CSV. Matt reached over and touched the end of my hair.

"I would hug you, but I'm much too sweaty from raking the yard," he said.

He was right. Sweat marks stained his shirt. Soil lodged between the straps on his sandals. And I was a neat freak repulsed by sweat, and dirt, and messy hair. But for whatever reason, it was all irresistibly attractive on Matt. He must have sensed it because he closed the short distance and gathered me into his arms. I felt a mass of rock-hard mass underneath his shirt, and every solid part made me weak in the knees. Matt held me close, and I felt his breath on my neck. My entire body relaxed and pinged awake at the same time.

A low woof interrupted us. Henry stood on the other side of the sliding glass door bonking his nose on the glass. *That was his signal.* We held each other a moment longer, then broke off the hug to let Henry outside. Henry walked right between us to the smoothly raked yard and squatted. Matt and I went back into the house to give him privacy, and I walked Matt to the front door.

"I'm going to get Bluebell and Stella. It's time for their exercise. Will you bring Henry and meet me across the street?"

I nodded. "Sure."

He paused. I was sure he was going to kiss me, desperately wished he would kiss me, silently ordered him to kiss me, but he didn't kiss me. I closed the door after he left, wondering why all the secondary characters were kissing me and the primary one wasn't.

Mrs. Bennet lounged in her usual spot with Snowball on her lap. The mass dynamics of the park were obvious, with Mrs. Bennet on one side of the park, everyone else on the other side. When I closed the inner gate after Henry, Gail waved me over. I searched down the dog run and spotted Grace and the Wilsons with a dark-haired woman. Was that Bob's wife? Other folks that had been in my living room congregated down there, too, but I hadn't spoken directly with any of them yet. Caroline entered the park right behind me, and Mrs. Bennet called out to both of us, waving us over with a vigorous arm. Caroline and I exchanged a glance before we strolled toward the wrought iron benches together.

"Better sit on that one." Gail indicated the bench across from her. "I'm still getting over a little something. I probably should have stayed in bed again, but I have my tea tomorrow, as you well know. Lots of committee actions happening. Carol, don't forget, you signed up to bake the brownies."

Caroline and I seated ourselves obediently, quietly.

"How's it going with Henry? Still giving you trouble?" Gail asked. "Did Micah leave that scooper for you? I asked him to stop by and see if you needed help with the poo."

That solved the mystery. M stood for Micah.

"Henry is a handful," I said simply. "Thank you very much for that scooper."

Gail passed me a small Ziploc bag of doggie treats.

"I also fixed up a little bag of these for you. Just give him two before leaving him alone and he'll behave, I guarantee it. Or three." She winked. "It's my special recipe. Dogs love them. They'll always behave if you give them the correct treats with a loving hand."

I accepted the treats gracefully and shoved them into my back pocket. For a moment, we stared across the park where the rest of the population had gathered. Most stood chatting, but Grace was doing jumping jacks and one man tossed balls for the dogs. George noisily entered the park with his large spotted dog. I stiffened at the sight of him, and he turned a hard face on our little group. Caroline waved at him, and his large spotted dog ran over to sit at attention in front of Mrs. Bennet, which seemed to annoy George.

"Looks like Bingo is begging for a treat," Mrs. Bennet said, pleased. She smirked at George, who had stepped over to us.

"Bengogh," George said. "His name is Bengogh. Good evening, ladies." I noticed he avoided eye contact with me.

Gail chuckled and gave the dog a treat. "Here you go, Bingo."

George still avoided facing me. Good, that meant he felt embarrassed. He should feel embarrassed. That meant he realized he was out of line. If he stayed embarrassed long enough, we might still have a chance to become friends. But not if he thought I'd fill a false prescription. I needed to ask

Doctor King about it. I wondered if we should report it. From across the park, a familiar growl reached our ears. I glanced at Henry, who was in his standard pose, belly in the dirt, head on his paws, staring at our little group. Was that growl coming from Henry?

George glanced at Henry, too, then his pale eyes flew to me for the very first time that evening. He took a few steps away from me and put his hands on his hips. Was he worried Henry would start running at him? He turned to Gail.

"So..."

But Gail Bennet shook her head slowly and pressed her lips at his inquiring eyes, and he turned away. He called Bengogh to follow him across the granite dog run to the other side of the park. I watched him give Henry the hound a sidelong look as he passed.

"Who was that growling a moment ago?" Caroline asked.

Neither Caroline nor Gail even suspected Henry. He still lay in the same position, the innocent little rascal. He was so adorable. After a moment, I noticed Caroline turn to Gail with a little hostility simmering in her expression. Gail glanced back, slightly amused.

"Did you file another complaint against Gatsby?" Caroline asked softly. "Eric got a call from animal control. They said you filed another complaint against our dog, a ridiculous complaint. Is that true? I thought we settled this. I thought this was over. I convinced Eric to back off."

Gail Bennet let her heavy feet smack to the ground, kicking up a little dust. She leaned forward, and I found her slightly menacing.

"Eric has not trained his dog," she said. "I know he's not walking him because he doesn't want to—"

"He's livid!" Caroline hissed under her breath.

"It's his own fault," Gail said and rubbed her nose with a tissue. "He promised to train Gatsby, and he's not trained. I know this has been a thorn in your side, but that husband of yours needs a good whipping, and I can see how it embarrasses you, the behavior. Eric thinks he knows best because he's a man, but maybe a little call from the authorities will open his eyes. Lord knows he won't listen to a female voice about anything. You tell Eric I'm not going away about this, or anything else, and I do consider it my business. I'm not the type to let this type of thing happen around me. He can't intimidate me."

Caroline glared at Gail. Normally, she appeared like a dignified lady, but at the moment, her face blazed red and her eyes burned fiercely. The whole effect shrank her.

"Did you hear about Joe? He died of a heart attack." Caroline said softly.

"He was an old man." Gail retorted just as softly.

"No one asked for your help," Caroline snapped. "Just know that whatever he does, it's your fault. Thank you so much for that, Gail."

Caroline stood up in a huff. Her dog followed obediently at the tone in her voice and the fence slammed behind her as they left. I turned back to Gail and was shocked to see her in distress. A trail of tears ran down her plump cheeks!

"Mrs. Bennet?"

She shook her head and wiped her eyes.

"Everyone always blames me when all I do is try to help." Gail took a deep breath and gathered her things. "No one knows, but that dog had cancer. Old Major was in terrible pain, and he had other diseases, too, his liver was bad. He should have been put down over a year ago. And old Joe, if he had a heart attack, it was his third. That man was a walking time bomb. Guess who called the ambulance that last time? Me. And I've got to tell you, he was not alive when I found him." Gail stood heavily. "And Caroline, next time you see her, you ask that woman who sheltered her for two days when that man decided to use her as a punching bag, and no number of threats from that man will make me back down. I won't have that behavior happening around me! Rule breakers and deadbeats, Sarah, don't listen to them, and don't get mixed up with them "

She left just as noisily as Caroline had. I sat stunned, watching her hurry down the street. My heart was pounding, wondering, *Was any of that true?*

Slowly, the folks on the other side of the dog park began to spread out. George remained on his side of the granite runway, but Grace meandered over at the same time Matt arrived. He had gone home not just to get his dogs, but I noticed he had showered and changed into fresh clothes. He grinned at me as he entered the park. He searched around and waved to the fellows on the far side of the runway.

"Another clean shirt," Grace chuckled softly.

Matt came round and joined us on the wrought iron benches. The dogs ran around him, and he threw the balls they delivered, but they kept coming back like moths attracted to a lamp. I knew exactly how they felt. I also felt drawn to him.

"Do you think Mrs. Bennet is coming?" he asked. "I thought she'd be here by now."

"You barely missed her, she came and went." Grace told him, then turned to me. "What went on down here anyway? I saw Caroline leave very upset and then Mrs. Bennet went off quickly, too. Did Caroline confront Gail? She said she was going to. What did Gail say?"

They both stared at me.

"She said Joe suffered three heart attacks, and his dog was terminal, basically."

Grace snorted. Matt's eyes darkened.

"Look at Bingo down there," Grace said. "See how he's sitting, not chasing balls like usual? I saw her. She gave him a treat. Just one. She puts something in the treats, I know it. Stacy, remember Stacy with the large bulldog?" She knocked on Matt's shoulder. "Stacy said those treats almost killed her dog. Gail gave her a small baggie of them to help train her dog to behave, but the dog didn't wake for over twenty-four hours. She was sure it was the treats."

Good grief! I pulled the treats out of my back pocket and held the small Ziploc bag up like it was hot and dangerous. There were several chunks of something in there, covered with a white powdery, sugar-like substance. I held them out, and Grace reached for them. Three dogs instantly came around and sat at attention. Grace's dog Mollie, a black Lab, and a smaller dog with triangle ears sticking straight up. They each had their eyes trained on that bag of treats. Grace tightened her grip on the bag, then stood up to keep it out of doggie reach. She shook her head at the three beggars.

"No!" she said sternly, chin pointing sharply, "No." She hid the bag under her shirt.

It took Matt throwing the tennis balls far away to get them to disperse, but for a short time, they would each bring back a ball and sit at attention in front of Grace. They knew she had the bag under her shirt.

"My god, what do you think she puts in these things?" Grace remained standing, staring down each dog who came up to her. She glanced at me. "Are you going to give them to Henry? I don't think you should. I'm certain she adds something to them, or on them. Look at how these fellows are desperate to get one. Joanne down there has plenty of treats, and she's giving them out freely. You don't see anyone sitting at attention for her. Gail Bennet must have mixed something good in these things."

Mrs. Bennet picked up a lot of different drugs in the past week. But those pills belonged to other people, right? People expected them. People right across the road in Heritage Park, the retirement community. Did Gail skim off some of their prescriptions? George implied that *she* had gotten the pills he wanted. Did she skim some of those pills to sell to George? Did Mrs. Bennet use part of those prescriptions to spike her doggie treats? *Trazodone.* Mrs. Bennet picked that one up on her last visit to CSV. Trazodone would put a dog to sleep, guaranteed. And she got plenty of opioids, dogs probably experienced the same pleasant sensations as humans with opioids. I wondered if any of the folks she picked up for noticed some of their pills missing. Did they count the pills like I counted the pills? Would Gail Bennet really drug a dog with stolen prescription medication?

"Do you want these back?" Grace asked. "If so, can I have one? I want to have it analyzed."

"You can have them all," I said. "I don't want them."

Grace nodded. "Karma is going to catch up to that old woman. I'm going to have these treats looked at. Or maybe I'll mix them in with a little sugar and flour and make her a nice treat of her own. See how she reacts to her own medicine. Maybe it'll put her to sleep for a few days and give us another long Bennet break out here." She laughed wickedly. Then, she called Mollie and ran down the crushed granite to meet her dog halfway and left. George followed soon after, disappearing in the same direction as Grace.

Other folks also trickled out of the park. The dinner hour was at hand, and there was always a lull in the park at that time. Matt suggested we sit a while longer and have a pizza delivered to my house. I thought that was a fine idea. He made the call and then switched benches to sit next to me. We faced the western sky and watched the colors change. It took several minutes for him to take my hand, and I found his golden-brown tiger's eyes staring into mine. But he still hadn't tried to kiss me, and I wondered why. I glanced down at his hand and at the small brown dots near his thumb. No infection, no rabies, he was safe.

"Do you think you are going to be okay with Henry tonight?" Matt asked softly. The hound dog lay half a dog park away under a tree. Matt's Labs had joined Henry, and all three of them sat staring at us from a distance, breathing hard with their tongues hanging out. Were they giving us privacy? "He seems so calm, it's hard to imagine him tearing up your stuff like that. But dogs do get their feelings hurt. He must be acting out about Josh leaving him. I wish I could take him for you, but..."

"We'll be fine. I'm not going to let you take Henry. There's not much more damage he can do at my place."

Matt did not look convinced, but the concern in his eyes did interesting things to my heart. Then, he finally did it. He leaned over and touched his lips to mine. A distinct electric pulse shot through my entire system. If I hadn't been sitting, I would have collapsed like an old-fashioned thumb puppet when the base is pushed in. My entire body vibrated with anticipation. The kiss never progressed past a chaste closed-lip mushing, but I was in love. I was sure of it, or at least in lust, it had to be one of those. Just when I had that thought, there was heavy panting around us.

The dogs had come closer. They were right at our knees, tongues hanging out, eyes excited and alert, and across the street, the pizza delivery guy was knocking heavily on my door, wondering why I wasn't answering. Matt stared at me, and we both giggled nervously. Then, he helped me stand, and we went off to have a romantic dinner of delivery pizza and wine. Thanks to George Johnson, there was still half a bottle of red tucked into the corner of my kitchen.

Over the course of a simple dinner under the romantic glow of doggy eyes, Matt kissed me one more time, on my hand. The dogs were on the back patio, sharing water and pig ear treats while watching the action at my kitchen table. Matt and I sat drinking wine and taking small bites of a vegetarian pizza from the Pizza Guys. Matt told me more about his former life living up near Seattle.

He had trained to be a forest firefighter and helped contain quite a few large fires in his day. But when things had taken a turn during his training and his sister's relationship fell apart, he agreed to move to California. He confessed the terrible thing he had gone through. He had gotten burned while in training, in the brush, during a wildfire. Even worse, his girlfriend at the time, Nancy, had also been burned. She had been training to be a firefighter, too. He felt guilty. Matt was the one who talked her into firefighting, encouraged her, and they were both maimed during training in a blaze that had gotten out of control.

"What happened to her, what happened to you," I told him, "you can't blame yourself."

He shook his head at me, like I didn't understand. Nancy recovered from her burns and continued her training, still determined to be a firefighter. Nancy was very tough. Matt recovered from his burns and ran away.

"I couldn't go back," he said. "And that ended things with Nancy. I couldn't face her again. I got scared and embarrassed that she was stronger than me."

He became terrified of fire and could not look Nancy in the eye during his phase of terror. She still lived up in Seattle and got engaged to one of the other fellows from their training class. They were both certified firefighters now, and Matt was still drifting. He turned hopeful eyes on me.

"But I'm feeling a surge of optimism lately. Like maybe I can finish my training and get back into it. Being a firefighter had always been my childhood dream. My father had been a firefighter, and California is a good place to be a firefighter, especially for wildfires. I'm looking into it."

He inquired about my background and wanted to know all about my past. An only child, now an orphan, a shy studious girl, temporarily displaced in Natomas, a dog park spy, not good at meeting new people, trying to take care of an animal for the first time in my life.

"Temporary?" His brow wrinkled with worry. "You mean, you aren't staying in Natomas? How long are you planning to be here?"

"I plan to live in California for three years unless I fall in love with the pharmacy and move back east this fall. CSV is a summer job, to test the waters and figure out if I might be happy as a pharmacist, or if I should go for that medical degree. My father, both my parents actually, hoped I'd become a medical doctor because they had been doctors. I diverted to pharmacy school because I was afraid of the cadaver lab and dealing with sick people, and…" And *because my father died*, I didn't add. There was no one to disappoint anymore. But I began thinking that maybe I had disappointed myself. Joe's lifeless body flashed into my head, and I suddenly worried if I was on the right track. Good grief, that incident left me seriously wondering again. I continued telling Matt my plan. "UC Davis agreed to accept a big chunk of my units from pharma school, and I'm slated to start the winter term out there. I might move closer to Davis, or I might stay in this house. If I get a car, I'll probably stay here. I've been thinking about getting a car."

I bet he wondered how I paid for all my schooling and the house. Besides being a good student, my parents left me a generous inheritance of old New England money. But sooner or later, I would have to settle down and focus on replenishing the family legacy. Matt's face became thoughtful and, unfortunately, less amorous. Maybe I said too much. We let the dogs inside, and Henry and I walked them to the door. Matt wore a serious expression on his face. What was he thinking? Was I too complicated for him? Just when I thought the night was over, it happened.

Matt kissed me again. A real kiss. A deep kiss. A knee-buckling, breathtaking, spontaneous kiss with a serious hug. I felt all the solid muscles under his nice shirt and melted into the solid strength of his arms, *the duke!* I felt his hands run up my rib cage and stop shy of being too forward. My thoughts swirled, just look at us, both rethinking our life paths. Both working past a fear that kept us from our real dreams. Both moving to Natomas to figure it all out. Surely, all those vectors had been pointing toward this perfectly passionate kiss.

Then, he left, and I closed the door and sighed. I turned to Henry and wondered what Henry thought about my kissing Matt, a guy I barely knew. Did Henry worry about these things, believe my behavior was not well thought out? Henry just blinked blankly at me.

"Oh, Henry," I said. "I'm not sure what to do with you. Where shall it be?" The hall, the backyard, the bathroom? Where would Henry do the least damage? "If you promise to be good, to just sleep and not get into any mischief, then maybe…"

Henry's tail moved. It slowly thump, thump, thumped behind him, and I laughed. I dragged his doggie bed into the master suite and placed it next to my king-sized bed. Henry climbed right into it and turned to watch me get ready. Then, I climbed into the blankets and lay my head on my pillow so I could see him. He lay with his head on his paws, drooling from the corners of his mouth, watching me. He was so funny. And sometime later, as we both stared into each other's eyes, I fell asleep.

# Day Six

## with Henry

I hit the snooze on my alarm, still drowsy and mostly asleep. I could feel myself drifting back into dreamland. But several waves rocked that boat, and they slowly shook me out of my stupor. I opened my eyes and found that Henry had climbed onto my bed. He was staring down at me and nudging me with his nose. I looked at the clock. *Good grief,* I must have hit the snooze ten times!

I sat up and patted Henry on the head. I massaged his sorrowful brow.

"Oh, Henry, I agree. It's much too early," I said. "But thank you for waking me up. And I'm going to tell you right now. No matter what I find when I walk around out there, I will try not to be angry. I might be falling in love, after all. And love and anger don't mix."

Henry obviously believed he lived with a hopeless romantic. He just lounged under my caressing hand and drooled all over my clean sheets. I let out a long sigh.

"Okay, let's see what the damage is."

There was no damage. The entire house looked good. Spare room, bathrooms, kitchen, living room, pantry, furniture, fixtures, closets, rugs, olive tree, nothing was out of sorts. I turned to Henry in astonishment. He sat on my favorite area rug and blinked at me. I rushed over and hugged him, rubbing behind his ears and trying to smooth out his thick wrinkles.

"Oh, Henry! You are such a good boy! Thank you, thank you, thank you for being a good boy!"

His only acknowledgment was a slight thumping of his tail. I had meant to do some yoga before work, but I woke up too late. Instead, I sat on my sofa, eating dry cereal and looking at the dog park. A man sat on Joe's bench, and that didn't seem right. Then, I glimpsed the boy who had helped with Henry's poop that first day. He strolled along the fence, letting his hand bounce along with the chain links. Then, a fast cyclist sped by. I watch George slow, turn, and coast up to the boy. Micah seemed to ignore George, but George jumped off his bike and stood in front of the boy, blocking his way. Good grief, what was he doing? I sat up to get a better view. Should I go outside? I stood up and opened the door.

"She can't cut me off!" George's voice carried through the cool morning air. "You tell the old bat to expect me at tea time today, and she'd better answer that door this time."

George glanced at my house and was stunned to see me watching them. He must have sensed me and Henry. He flashed a smile and a wave, then he hopped on his bike and sped away looking embarrassed. Micah also retreated. He had turned around and ran in the opposite direction. I looked down at Henry.

"That was extremely suspicious."

Henry just blinked and settled back onto the area rug.

I did not have a doggie door, but I did have a torn and faulty screen door. So, I explained to Henry that I would leave him in the house with the screen door blocking the yard, and the torn-out section could be his doggy door. The weather report said it would be a very hot day, so I was depending on him not to do any more territory marking or structural damage inside the house. I promised to come home for lunch and check on him. Henry just lay on his rug watching me talk, blinking and drooling and breathing loudly.

That morning, the CSV pharmacy buzzed with activity. Many new prescriptions came down the pipe with some needing special preparation. Two orders for mixers, both pediatric liquid antibiotics that would take a bit of time and care. A highly viscous suspension would better ensure proper dosages could be administered, but too high a viscosity would be hard for a young kid to swallow. Liquid antibiotics were always tricky to mix. I didn't want to hurry, but I hoped to peruse the computer and jot down the names of one or two of the folks Gail Bennet fetched meds for. I got it in my head to visit them. I was worried. What if Gail skimmed medications and sold pills to fellows like George Johnson?

About two hours into my morning shift, Doctor King tapped me on the shoulder. He indicated I should take a short break. He glanced over his glasses at me with an interesting look in his eye.

"I think you better come and see this," he said.

He hummed under his breath as he led me back to the small office where a vase full of flowers decorated my desk. A beautiful, colorful array of asters, small roses, and violets brightened the room. It was a spectacular arrangement, a perfect assortment. Good grief, I was not prepared for a vase full of flowers. My heart swelled astronomically. I absolutely loved love. Never had flowers been delivered to my work place before. Granted, I never had a regular job before, but still! Doctor King nodded at me, pleased.

"Somebody is a smart fellow," he said and left me to my flowers.

I took the small card and flipped it open. My elation immediately deflated.

*I'm sorry for anything Henry's done. Please let me make it up to you when I return. My friend Troy will pick him up soon. Love, Josh.*

Ugh! No! I felt extremely disappointed the beautiful bouquet did not come from Matt. The arrangement did not look half as spectacular as it did a moment ago.

When I uncharacteristically ran out to lunch, Doctor King probably thought I was running off to meet the flower sender. Well, he wasn't too far off the mark. I was running off to meet the flower sender's dog. The temperature was pretty hot and the fast walk home made me a little woozy. I still felt disappointed the flowers were not from Matt. I flew into the house and spotted Henry on the area rug right where I left him. I glanced around. Nothing was amiss. I quietly went from room to room to make sure there wasn't hidden chaos somewhere. I didn't want Henry to think I was checking up on him, but I needed to make sure everything was okay and it was. So, I made a peanut butter and jelly sandwich and sat on the floor next to Henry. I told him all about the pretty flowers Josh sent.

"I'm sure he meant them more for you than for me," I said to Henry. "He misses you."

Another prescription for the Heritage Park community popped into the system for Jane Bennet to pick up and deliver. But she called Doctor King and told him she was busy with her tea party and to expect her late, or even the next day. It was perfect, maybe I could deliver the medications instead. Heritage Park was just over Truxel Road from my place.

"Mrs. Bennet probably shouldn't deliver medicine to the old folks' community right now. I noticed she was under the weather, sniffling. Maybe I could do it. It isn't a problem."

Doctor King shook his head and put the medication on the wait-shelf. "No, no need to do that. Mrs. Bennet is the med runner on these, and it'll keep for a day, plus, this one's a recurring order and doesn't need to be rushed. Deliveries are a little below our pay grade," he winked at me.

*Xanan, Ativan, and Valium* for an Eleanor Vance. Funny name, I thought I'd heard it before. Did I meet her at the dog park by chance? Why does Eleanor need so many pills for anxiety? Was she the nervous type?

Caroline dropped into the CSV just after noon. She needed to pick up her *suvorexant*, a very strong sleep aid. She moved nervously, fidgety, and I watched Doctor King help her at the counter while I counted pills on the other side of the glass wall. When she turned her head toward me, her smile looked painful, and her wave was a delayed action. I couldn't see her eyes through the large dark sunglasses she wore. Two boxes of Betty Croker Supreme Chocolate Chunk Brownie mix sat on the counter next to her pills. Poor Caroline. She needed chocolate and was having sleepless nights. I thought about the terrible gossip that spilled out of Mrs. Bennet the previous day, and my anxiety began to skyrocket, but I slowly walked toward Caroline anyway. She noticed my approach and knew she couldn't escape without looking weird. Doctor King grinned at me and winked as he went into the back room.

"Hello, Sarah," Caroline sounded upbeat. "Nice to see you."

"Hi, Caroline." I could see the purple skin behind her sunglasses as I approached. Then, I said bluntly. "Are you okay?"

That wiped the smile off her lips, and she pressed them together instead.

"I'm sorry, but Mrs. Bennet mentioned… I just wanted to be sure you're okay. If you need a friend or someone to talk to, or… You're always welcome at my house. It's right across from the…" I was rambling like a total idiot. I didn't know what to say, or how to say it, or what to do. "You know where it is. I am so sorry if I am butting my nose in somewhere, but I just wanted to let you know that you're welcome at my house. Mrs. Bennet said that maybe… that you once needed a place to stay and…"

"Mrs. Bennet." Caroline interrupted in a low, stern voice. "What a mouth on that woman. You think she wants to help, but she's just stirring the pot. She's a devil in disguise, and I'm fine, thank you. She's holding court again, right now. She sent Micah to demand I come over to make peace and bring the brownies. I hope she gets too busy or tired and stays away from the dog park today. The other day out there, we had peace. Didn't we have peace that day, without her?"

She gathered up her pills and brownie mix and nodded to me. The line of her mouth bent in a brief, weak crescent before she turned away, and her feathered blond hair flowed beautifully as she moved. I wondered when her husband blackened that eye. How could a man manage to do that to his wife? I recalled when he arrived to pick her up at Swabbies. My first impression of him was of a mild-mannered very average man, balding on top, pudgy in the middle, polite but slightly annoyed at having to pick her up. They seemed mismatched, glamorous, witty Caroline with a quiet, mousy him. He barely greeted anyone, and I imagined he was shy, like me.

Despite Doctor King's pooh-pooing the idea, the urge to deliver the pills to Mrs. Vance felt overpowering. The Heritage Park care facility and housing development was just down the street from my house, a short jaunt over the canal and Truxel Road, right on my way home.

That entire community was gated, locked, and blocked by a giant apartment building, so I went into the main building to enter the premises. The folks on Gail Bennet's delivery list noted the main care facility as their primary residence, so they likely had rooms in that apartment complex. The entry lounge had several nice sofas and chairs, and offered a very nice gathering place for people to visit. That large room was painted in pastel colors, and a few animated groups sat chatting in scattered clumps. Across the way, I spotted a large open desk and a young woman fiddling with her cell phone. She glanced at me, and I quickly walked over to her smiling face.

"Are you visiting someone today?" she asked.

"Yes," I said. "I have some medications to deliver. The regular delivery woman, Jane Bennet, is out sick. I work at the pharmacy down the street and thought I'd bring them over myself."

"Oh," She appeared confused. "Okay."

"I'm dropping off meds for," I double-checked the name, "Eleanor Vance. I'm not familiar with her room number. Shall I take them there, or do we call her to come down here?"

"I don't know," the woman said. "It's a little unusual because we have an in-house pharmacy down in the clinic. Most residents get their medications delivered there. It's a wholesale distributor, directly linked to the med center. I don't know why she chose to go outside the system. Who did you say you were delivering for?" The woman started typing on her computer.

"Eleanor Vance," I said.

She chuckled and stared at me. "Better check the name again. It wasn't Eloise Vincent, was it? That old lady is very popular."

I looked at the name. "No, Eleanor Vance."

Her face was amused confusion. She studied me closely. "I don't have a list of everyone in the outdoor housing section, but I definitely know there isn't an Eleanor Vance in the main care building," she said. "Maybe she's a guest of someone out there in self-care housing."

"Maybe," I turned and glanced around the lobby. "How about one of these other folks? The med runner also delivers for them. I wonder if any of them live in the care building." I pulled out my folded list and read off the names. "Elizabeth Lavenza, John Seward, Justine Moritz, or Lucy Westenra. Do any of those people reside in the care building?"

Now the woman was full-on grinning and chuckling at me. She had beautiful hazel eyes and a bubbling, contagious laugh that shook her whole body.

"Did somebody put you up to this?" she asked. "Mr. Henderson perhaps? He's such a joker. Tell him he left out

Peter Quint, my personal favorite." Her eyes were full of mirth as she winked. "Are you related to him? I just adore him and his *bookworm* quizzes." She made the visual quotes signal with her fingers when she said bookworm. "Is he testing me again?"

The pretty young receptionist was laughing, but I was not.

After a few minutes more, I surmised that Mr. Henderson was a retired literature teacher who hosted a book club and discussion session with his fellow elders at the care facility. For the past few years, they had been focusing on classic horror fiction. Titles by Stoker, Shelley, Poe, Jackson, James, and Bradbury were all on the reading list. Mr. Henderson loved creating short quizzes for the bookworm club and had been trying to entice the woman behind the counter to join in the meetings, always leaving her a copy of the group's current classic horror novel. And though the woman did not know Jane Bennet, she did know *Gail*. Gail Bennet brought treats once a month to the care facility and often joined the book club meetings. Gail Bennet was always a riot.

I left feeling like a complete idiot and overbrimming with more anxiety. What should I do? Obviously, those names were supporting characters from books, just like Jane Bennet herself. Now that she said it, of course, I knew Eleanor Vance! Of course, she would need all that anxiety medication after the *Haunting at Hill House*! I was furious. I wanted to confront Gail Bennet right then and there. She lived a few blocks away from my house, next to the elementary school, and I could walk there easily. Instead, I called the pharmacy back office and spoke with Doctor King. I told him the Eleanor Vance prescription was a ruse along with several others. After a long pause, his voice sounded completely astounded. At first, he denied Mrs. Bennet could be a fraud, but he huffed that he would tag all of the prescriptions Jane Bennet ferried and call for an investigation.

"If this is true, it is quite unbelievable. Are you sure? Who did you speak with? Did you get a name?" Doctor King asked harshly. Then, mild-mannered Doctor King raised his voice. "If this is true," he knew it was true, "I can't believe it! That woman has been coming in here for over a year and looking me in the eye…" He became speechless as his voice cracked. "Please do not speak of this to anyone, Doctor Fitzgerald. We need to start an official investigation."

I raced toward my house, frantic to escape from view and to try to calm myself down. I took deep breaths, long breaths in, long breaths out. Henry lifted his head when I burst through door and watched me rush down the hall. I locked the undelivered meds in my closet safe with a shaky hand. I could use one of those pills but gripped my teardrop lepidolite instead. Quiet fury hovered below my surface. Did Doctor King worry his reputation was shot or his license at stake? It probably was. He was the lead pharmacist and calling for an investigation on his own mistake couldn't be easy for him. Was falsifying prescriptions common or uncommon?

After I calmed down, I strolled back toward Henry and paused to pat him on the head. Then, I slipped into the kitchen to fill up his water bowl and sat at the table to watch him drink. I tried to read a book, to put the situation out of my mind, but it was no use. I had a burning desire to speak to Gail Bennet in private, not at the dog park, and I needed to catch her before she left her house for the park. I wanted to look around her home to see if those drugs were lying on a counter somewhere. I admit, I also imagined slapping her right in the face.

I apologized to Henry and told him I needed to run one last errand before taking him across the street. It wouldn't take long. I needed to drop in on Gail and confront her. I would never be able to sit still if I didn't. *Rule breakers and deadbeats*! The nerve of her! That hypocrite!

Gail Bennet's house was painted a light canary color with off-white trim. Colorful, flowering bushes were planted along her front wall and stone walk. In the center of her clipped grass, a small squatting dog sign with "NO!" written in the body of the dog stuck out at an angle. Potted, hanging vines swayed on her front porch with some of the tendrils grabbing the stucco walls. A large wind chime hung limply from a hook on the corner of the patio. I stomped heavily up to the door before I noticed it.

Her cheerful yellow door was cracked open, and that little sliver of space sparked a feeling of Déjà vu to manifest in my system, and I hesitated. *Damn her!*

I rang the bell despite my beating heart.

I heard a high-pitched yelping in the house, Snowball.

I rang the bell again.

The yelping moved right to the other side of the door. Snowball's nose stuck out of the crack. He yelped and growled and barked in rapid succession. His nose poked in and out of the door, and I took a step backward, the fight draining right out of me.

I no longer wanted to confront Mrs. Bennet.

I no longer cared if she was a hypocrite.

Let someone else slap her.

But Snowball nudged the door and it swung wide open so that I glimpsed right into her personal world. A knitted throw covered the back of a velvet green love seat. A curio cabinet in the corner, against a wall, contained multiple figurines that might be different versions of Snowball. An upright piano with the keys uncovered had complicated sheet music on the stand and a large metronome on the piano top board. Photographs of people were scattered around that living room, smiling and hugging in black and white and in color. I spotted the photo of a man in a military outfit standing at attention. On the coffee table, a tea set was left out, and one of the cups had overturned with the spilled-out contents on the floor. On a large plate, there were brownies and other pastries. I peered deeper into the house but saw nothing move except Snowball.

Snowball jumped up and down like a little maniac. He ran a very quick circle around the living room, upsetting a framed photo, then stopped to look at me with bulging eyes. My heart raced faster than his little feet.

"Mrs. Bennet?" I called meekly into the house.

Snowball ran deeper into the house. I could hear the pitter-patter of his feet, and his yelps and barks went loud, then faint, then loud again. *I should call the authorities and wait outside for them to arrive.* But what if Gail needed help? What if she needed to be turned on her side, or her head elevated, or have direct pressure applied to a bleeding wound, or chest compressions, or her airway cleared? What should I do? Matt had walked right into a strange house to check on Joe. Life or death often meant action over inaction. One minute could save a life and so I stepped into the house. *Rulebreaker,* her voice echoed in my ear. *Please don't let me find a dead body,* I begged the universe. The pounding blood muffled my ears, and the air in Mrs. Bennet's home closed in on me.

I tentatively stepped deeper into the house. Snowball zipped around my legs, pausing once to look at me and bark. His eyes appeared crazed. Then, he zipped away, and I followed him. He went into the kitchen. It was a mess, white powder everywhere, small paw prints zig-zagged through it. I noticed the sugar bowl tipped over, also the flour jar, everything was mixed together, and Snowball lapped it up with his tiny pink tongue. His beady eyes practically popped out of his head. Was he high on sugar?

"Mrs. Bennet!" I called down the hall. "Mrs. Bennet! Are you here? Are you okay? Please answer me," my voice cracked.

I slowly tip-toed down the hall, shaking, pulse off the charts, my vision tunneling. I was already inside the house without permission, I just needed to do a quick check before leaving. I ordered myself to calm down. *Please don't let me find a dead body!* She probably just stepped outside to a neighbor's house. *Yeah, right.* Snowball zipped past me. He ran in and out of all the rooms, crisscrossing in front of my slow steps. He disappeared into the last room down the hall, and by the sound of his yelping and barking and growling, I knew that was the room holding the jackpot, that everything interesting would be in that back room. I turned the corner and saw them.

Mrs. Bennet was sprawled across the bed with Snowball standing right on top of her. Snowball jumped up and down on her chest, barking, growling, yelping, and *biting.* He was nipping at her. Biting her nose and ears and neck. *Good Grief! Gross! Please, stop!* I almost turned tail and ran away, or fainted, but instead, I screamed. Snowball stopped momentarily and stared at me with his crazy, bulging marble eyes. He bared his teeth and growled at me.

I ran into the room and smacked him off Mrs. Bennet. He went tumbling off the bed, landed on the floor, rolled, recovered, and started toward me. I kicked him across the room, and he slid into the bathroom. I know it was an unfair fight. I had at least a 125-pound advantage on that little mutt, but his teeth looked razor-sharp, and his eyes seemed demonic, and my adrenaline was sky-high.

I ran over and slammed the bathroom door shut, trapping him. I heard myself panting, dizzy, wanting to faint. I fumbled with my phone as I turned back to Mrs. Bennet. Was she alive? Was she dead? Then, I saw her eyes. They were wide open. *Rule breaker.* I was face to face with another corpse, my worst fear. I could hear myself speaking to the 911 operator, gasping between words. My voice sounded oddly strained and high-pitched, crazy. I could barely catch my breath. I didn't know anything. I just knew the street name, but I quickly forgot it, so I didn't know the name after all. And the house color might be yellow, or black, or yellow, but it felt black, very, very black. I definitely knew that there was a crazy dog in the bathroom, or maybe he was possessed. I could barely see anything except for a small area right in front of me. I touched Mrs. Bennet's neck. Spongy, cool, and calm, and her body already had a slightly deflated look about her. *I can't breathe, was it really her, did somebody hide the real body?* A thick cake of dried foam coated her lips and nostrils. She was definitely dead. She was not making any more bubbles.

"It's right next to Regency Park Elementary School," I whispered into the phone.

I ran outside to get sick in Mrs. Bennet's beautiful flowering hedges, then I crumbled onto her front step to wait for the authorities. I kept my head between my knees, trying to slowly inhale and then exhale steadily, but something had sucked all of the oxygen out of the atmosphere. I felt like I was gasping.

I wasn't sure how I got home. The nice police officer with the firm and gentle grip must have escorted me. He gave off a nice, calming scent that reminded me of my father and made me feel safe. I knew somewhere back there, I vomited, but somehow my breath smelled minty fresh. Someone had given me mint gum, probably that policeman after he fed me a bottle of water.

He came into my house and fed Henry two scoops of food without asking, then he went out to my small backyard and used the pooper scooper to clean up after Henry. Back inside, he put on the kettle and brewed some tea, saying something about my Brown University mug. He covered me with my throw as I sat on my damaged sofa. Then, he wrote out his personal phone number, just in case, on a small square of paper. He planned to hang around Regency Park until the end of his shift at midnight. If I needed anything, if I remembered anything, if I just wanted to talk, he would drive right over. I didn't remember his name, but on the paper, he had scribbled a sloppy *Officer Shane Bane* next to a slanted phone number. Was he lefthanded? My father had been lefthanded. He told me a detective might drop by the next day, and I should probably stay home from work. He waited for several minutes to be sure I locked the door behind me. I heard him telling folks outside that there was nothing to see and to go away.

Henry stood and stared at me. We were very overdue for the dog park that evening. He was probably wondering what had taken so long. I had said it would be little errand, but I had been gone a very long time. I turned off all the lights. Instead of sitting on the couch, I slid down to the ground onto Henry's little area rug. I didn't want anyone in the dog park to see me in the window. As I sank to the ground, Henry strolled over and put his large head on my lap. He moved in close and covered me with his mass. I bent over and hugged him as the tears finally streamed down my face.

And to think I rushed over there to give her a piece of my mind. I wondered who would contact all the people in those photos. What would they say? I wondered how she died. Did she overdose on the drugs I gave her? I felt responsible for what I had seen.

"Oh, Henry," I whispered into a large floppy ear. "I was fooled by those names, Jane Bennet, George Wickham, and my stupid wish. I thought I stumbled into a romance story. But it's really a horror story, isn't it? I missed all the clues. It's just not my genre." I searched his melancholy eyes and truly believed Henry had known all along. Dogs always knew more than we gave them credit for. Then, Henry scooted closer and pinned me with his weight, he knew I needed it. Henry and I both fell asleep in the living room that night, me on the sofa, him on his rug.

# Day Seven

## with Henry

A loud knocking woke me up. Henry was already awake and sat alert, watching the front door. He stared at it with a low growl under his breath. I stood up and glanced out the window, but my window did not allow me to see who was on my small porch knocking. I felt hungover and had a terrible headache.

"Sarah, are you in there?" It was George Johnson. "Sarah."

"Go away," I said to the door.

"I wanted to say I'm sorry. About the other morning." He lowered his voice. "And I wanted to stop by..."

"Go away," I said. Henry barked loud and low.

From the front window, I watched George finally retreat. He stared at my house but thankfully could not see me. Why had he come? Was he after gossip? Was he afraid about the drugs? *Did he knock on Gail Bennet's door yesterday?* He positioned his small helmet on his red head with his eyes fixed on my window. Then, he stepped onto his bike and clipped his shoes onto the pedals before he sped off.

I had a ton of messages, mostly from Doctor King at the CSV. I called and listened to his shaky instructions. For the next few days, the CSV pharmacy would be closed. The police already informed him of what I stumbled upon the previous evening. A detective visited the CSV bright and early, and our investigation into the Jane Bennet drug fiasco was put on hold. The death of Gail Bennet complicated it. The police asked Doctor King all sorts of questions about me. They found a drug container in her home from CSV with a name other than Gail Bennet on it. I felt bad for Doctor King, his voice sounded very old and weak.

"I still have the medications for Eleanor Vance," I said softly. "I doubt she exists."

"Just secure them," his voice was a whisper. "We'll recover them later. Maybe later today you can... or I can... We'll worry about them later."

Henry and I stayed home. We did silent stretches in front of the couch. Henry's yoga efforts were very cute, and he successfully made me laugh more than once. Henry attempted to mimic every yoga position I made, except the upside-down tripod lotus challenge. I didn't blame him. Then, there was another sharp rap on the door. Who? I peeked out the peephole. A man in a tucked-in green polo shirt and slacks had taken a step back from the door so I could see him easily. He looked harmless. I opened the door a crack. I noticed the few folks in the dog park staring at my front door and this little interaction. The man's smile did not reach his eyes.

"Hello, Sarah Fitzgerald?"

I nodded, "Yes, are you the detective?"

My question confused him, and his face tensed up. "No, no. My name is Troy McClure, a friend of Josh's. He asked me to pick up Henry. I came around last night, but you didn't answer the door." He glanced at his cell phone, then back at me. "I don't have a lot of time, but I can take him if you like. I know how destructive that dog can be. I babysat Henry once, and he did a number on my game room. Tore up my pool table."

I stared at Troy McClure. Neat polo shirt, nicely combed black hair, belted khaki pants, steady dark eyes, annoyed expression. He definitely belonged in pharma sales. Maybe he was one of Josh's colleagues. He tried to smile again, but the line of his mouth couldn't pull it off. I believed he wasn't very happy about fetching Henry.

"Josh sounded pretty desperate. I think he's afraid Henry has wrecked things for you two. Henry is an odd dog.

The only person Henry hasn't terrorized is Stan, the last person to watch him. But Stan is away right now, too."

I glanced at Henry, relaxing on his area rug. He watched me from under his hooded eyes, waiting. *Two good nights.* Henry had been an easy dog for two nights. Was it a tease? Would he suddenly turn into a wrecking ball again, or had we finally come to an understanding?

"Aren't you afraid he'll damage your game room?" I asked softly.

Troy chuckled and grinned wickedly. "I rented a crate. I'm not taking any chances with him."

He planned on putting Henry into a crate. *Good grief!* Here was my chance to unload my Henry headache, but did I still have a Henry headache? That drool was not half a gross as it had been a few days ago, and I did not want Henry put into a crate over it, especially with this man who obviously disliked him. Somehow, I wanted Henry to stay. The house would feel so empty without him, and Henry made me feel… safe.

"I changed my mind," I said. "I'll keep him here." Then I shut the door on his gaping face.

Next came the detective. No polo shirt or khaki pants, the detective wore a real shirt with real slacks, formal shoes, a tie, a jacket with patches on the elbows like an old English professor. I wondered if he knew the name of Doctor Frankenstein's fiancé or that doctor from the mental institute in Dracula. *So many doctors in horror stories.* He was much older than Officer Shane Bane, and he kept his badge in his wallet like a detective in a movie. Detective Allen.

I confirmed that Gail Bennet was a med runner for CSV and went by the name Jane. As she was sick, I decided to deliver some pills for her. I didn't suspect her of forging the prescription at first, that came later. I reported my suspicions immediately, he could confirm that with Doctor King. There should be a phone record of it in the pharmacy log. Yes, I only started working at the pharmacy last month. Yes, I'm familiar with giving injections and had recently administered a tetanus vaccination to someone. Yes, I moved into the neighborhood recently, last month and hardly knew anyone. Yes, I met Gail Bennet at the dog park.

"Why did you go to Mrs. Bennet's home yesterday?" the detective asked.

"I was angry with her," I said.

He looked surprised at my answer.

"I was furious and wanted to confront her," I admitted. "She acted like my friend, but she was lying to me. I felt like a fool, about the Eleanor Vance prescription, and I wanted to tell her off." *And slap her,* I didn't add.

The detective stared into my eyes, studying my face. He had dark brown-grey hair with wild brown-grey eyebrows and a large mustache. A few of those eyebrow hairs stuck up haphazardly in odd directions. He reminded me of the photo of Mark Twain on the back of a book jacket in my father's study.

"You admit you were angry at Gail Bennet and went to her house to confront her?"

"Yes," I said. "I was very, very angry."

"You were upset at how she beat the system at CSV? Upset at what type of repercussions it might have for you and Doctor King?"

"Oh, yes. This is horrible for us."

His lips pressed together.

"Did she overdose on something she got from CSV?"

He flipped a page in his small notebook. He drained the cup of coffee I had given him, and when he glanced back at me, his eyes had softened.

"I can't say how she died because this is an ongoing investigation," he said. "Do you happen to know a kid named Micah? Maybe have an idea of where he lives?"

"I only met him once. He does odd jobs for Mrs. Bennet... did odd jobs. Someone said he lives in the apartments over there." I pointed to the north.

He nodded and jotted notes with a fat pen.

"I should let you know that her death was not an accident. This is a suspicious death investigation."

What did that mean? Gail Bennet was murdered? Killed? Did I miss something? Had there been a knife wound, a bullet wound? I didn't see any blood. Maybe she was strangled. But she had dried foam on her lips and nose, so poisoned? *Drug-related.* Forced overdose? His eyes were studying me, and my heart started pounding again.

"Am I a suspect?"

"Right now," he said, "everyone is a suspect."

Henry and I went across the street to the dog park. We waited for someone familiar to go in, Isabella with the patched shepherd mix dog, and then we went right over, and I sat across from her. She was excited to see me and wanted to talk. It was human nature. A tragic event occurred, and people needed to talk about it. Isabella told me that Grace had knocked on my door the previous night, but I didn't answer. People were concerned about me. By people, she meant Caroline and Matt and Grace and George among others. Isabella leaned toward me.

"They say the dog was eating her," she whispered.

I closed my eyes on the image her words conjured up and shook my head. "I think he was just nipping. Maybe he was trying to wake her."

Luckily, Matt clanked into the park. He hurried over, and I stood up to receive a much-needed hug. There was a reason why men were so tall and solid with strong arms. I soaked up his embrace, not caring that Isabella beamed with interest in the whole affair. Matt slipped in a brief kiss on my forehead, then we sat down together on one of the benches.

"The police suspect foul play," I told them gently. "I'm a suspect."

Isabella gasped and shrunk away, studying me with wide fearful eyes. I didn't blame her, she barely knew me, and I'd recently found two dead bodies. Matt glanced sideways at Isabella.

"It's normal, she found the body, I bet everybody around here is a suspect."

I nodded. "The detective did say everyone is a suspect."

"Everyone?" Isabella's dark eyes flashed indignantly. "I don't think so. Nobody better tell me I'm a suspect. I only ever talked to her out here, I hardly even know her! I'm not a suspect. I certainly never went to any of those tea parties she hosted. I refuse to be a suspect!"

More people than usual filed into the park, and they all seemed to be whispering gossip about dead Mrs. Bennet and the police activity surrounding her house. Lots of folks were surprisingly well informed after just a short amount of time. An online neighborhood chat site floated all the inside information. I listened to the gossip as it shot back and forth over my head.

The authorities ransacked the Bennet house all through the night with bright lights and mystery vans in the driveway and on the street. Police tape was still draped across her door and stretched over her yard, and the whisperers insisted it was a major a crime scene. The police questioned folks in the early morning, and they obtained a list of visitors they were interested in. Apparently, Mrs. Bennet hosted a tea every other Wednesday between ten and two. Her tea party socials were her way to touch base with several folks in the different clubs she headed. The neighborhood watch, the charity food drive, the yard patrol to name a few. Someone asked Matt if he had visited Gail, but Matt generically shook his head, not confirming or denying a visit. The police were actively searching for the young boy, Micah. Several people reported seeing Micah run in and out of Gail Bennet's house more than once the previous day.

Several people crowded around our bench, and I had to consciously breathe slowly to allay my nerves. The voices sounded more excited than distressed, and that disturbed me. Joe and Gail both had been distinct fixtures at the dog park, and now they were both suddenly gone. That had to affect everyone who came into the dog park, but why did they sound so excited? Then, Caroline strolled into the park. She glanced at our small crowd and waved, but she avoided the gathering and went to Joe's old bench instead. Caroline still wore those large sunglasses and her head jerked about like she might be looking for someone. Isabella weaved through the crowd to hurry toward Caroline. A man I did not know filled the spot on the bench she had left and shimmied over close to me. I tried to shrink away and felt very much like asking people to back off. The crowd made me feel claustrophobic and I searched around for an opening to make an escape of my own.

"They say the dog was rabid." That man next to me added to the gossipy slander. "Is that true? On *Next Door* someone said her little dog had to be restrained with a muzzle by animal control, and he was a rabid, crazy dog."

"Did Snowball kill her?" someone else wondered. "I never liked that little dog."

A few people felt certain the small dog was responsible for Gail Bennet's death.

"You were in the house." A woman behind me added softly. "Do you think the dog was rabid? They say he might have picked it up at the shelter, from Old Major."

I shook my head. "Maybe he was high on too much sugar. I saw him licking it up in the kitchen when I got there. The sugar bowl had been knocked over."

The man beside me snorted loudly, stifling a laugh. Everyone glanced at him. He shrugged and stood up. Thank goodness he was going away.

"She didn't keep sugar in that bowl." He nodded knowingly at the crowd. "That dog was high on cocaine or some other stimulant. She was a drug dealer, right? I heard she kept cocaine in the sugar bowl."

Matt stared at him. "Let's not start any rumors."

"It's not a rumor," the man said. "She was a dealer, and Micah was her errand boy, and part of her tea parties were nice little drug exchanges. It's not a secret what she kept in that sugar bowl. Or in that flour jar. Or in those little packets of 'spice'. Seriously, the police must already know what's in those jars. It is all over *Next Door*. I admit it, I got pain killers from her, in a spice packet, last year. Remember when my back went out and my doctor suggested Motrin? That goddamn idiot. Gail Bennet saved my back, yes, she did. Plus, someone's cousin's brother works at the station and he's posting everything, he would know."

The gossip was certainly flying around us. People hovered closer to me, and I began to feel closed in again. I didn't know how to escape that crowd without coming in contact with too many bodies. I glanced at Matt, but he was listening intently to all the gossip. Did these people squeeze in so closely because they hoped I'd start spilling more details? I felt like they were trying to get me to say something.

Two policemen entered the park and stared at our group. I noticed Officer Shane Bane and flashed on a memory of him carrying me and putting me into the back of a police car. He had a gentle voice and I remembered staring at the pores of his neck and feeling safe. The two officers meandered around slowly, greeting people, and Officer Bane gravitated toward me and Matt on the bench. The police had quite a repulsive effect on the gossip, and I felt relief as people dispersed, allowing me to breathe again. Officer Bane flashed a reserved smile, and I noticed part of his bulk must be a Kevlar vest hidden underneath his dark blue police shirt. He must be terribly hot but gave off the appearance of being cool and comfortable. His steady eyes flickered over every person in the dog park before settling back on me, studying me.

I couldn't remember if I thanked him for helping me home the previous evening. I recalled a steady, quiet voice coaxing me to calm down, and I felt slightly shy with his eyes still fixed on my face. Did he think I was mixed up with the wrong crowd and possibly a killer?

"Nice to see you looking better, Doctor Fitzgerald." He shifted his attention to Henry in the shade and he had a twinkle in his eye for him. "That's a real hound dog you have over there, a true bloodhound. He's very handsome and in excellent shape."

"Yes, thank you," I said, but I didn't know the difference between a bloodhound or any other type of hound dog. I still felt embarrassed about the vomit and anything I might have said or did. I felt myself correcting my posture in front of the officer, sitting up straighter.

Matt stood up to shake the officer's hand and to introduce himself. The two men stood face to face and spread out their bulks. The Kevlar vest and bulky belt of tools gave Officer Bane a little advantage. Officer Bane looked neat and tidy in his pressed uniform and perfect gig line. The buttons of his shirt were all aligned with his belt buckle and trouser flap, and his shoes were polished to a high reflective shine. He spoke in a soft formal tone, unlike Matt with his casual familiarity. Matt came across as carefree, wild, and passionate in his sandals and shorts compared to the stiff policeman's rigid posture. For a brief moment, Matt looked like a silly boy next to the police officer.

"Do either of you happen to know if a woman named Grace is in the park right now? A woman with a golden retriever?" Officer Bane inquired.

"No, she's not here," Matt told him. "Is she in trouble?"

"Oh, no, no." Officer Bane assured him. "We want to touch base with her. Maybe ask her a few questions. Do you happen to know her last name or where she lives?"

I shook my head quietly.

"Her last name is Briar," Matt told the officer. "George would know where she lives." Matt pointed to George, who arrived earlier without my notice. He stood on the other side of the park throwing balls for Bengogh. "That guy over there, with the red hair. I think they used to date."

Officer Bane thanked him for the information and shook his hand. He nodded to me again, then turned toward George Johnson. Did Officer Bane wonder if I killed Mrs. Bennet? I couldn't tell. He had been eyeing me oddly during that entire exchange. I could feel Matt standing nervously next to me and caught him with a pensive expression on his face. Did Matt also wonder if I might possibly have killed Mrs. Bennet? We hardly knew each other.

"You still have Henry. I thought he'd be gone by now." Matt said. "Last night a fellow stopped by when you weren't answering the door. He said was coming back today."

"I changed my mind," I said. "He was going to put Henry in a crate."

Matt nodded. "Henry has been a pretty bad dog. I hope he doesn't lapse; dogs can be unpredictable."

Was he implying that I should have allowed Troy to put Henry in a crate? That couldn't be what he meant. Perhaps he was worried Henry would cause more destruction, and I would be upset again. Maybe he thought I could use one less distraction with everything that was going on. We watched as Officer Shane Bane approached George.

"I'm sorry, but I need to get going," Matt said suddenly. "I wish I could keep you company, but I have to get the Labs home and… I have a work thing due tonight." He rubbed his hands over his messy hair. "Maybe we can have lunch tomorrow. Can I take you to lunch tomorrow? Maybe we can get away from some of this."

After Matt left, Isabella returned to my bench. She called her mixed shepherd Rosie and hooked her leash to the collar. Isabella glanced past me, to where Officer Shane Bane and George were laughing together. That policeman appeared good at making people feel at ease and he had very good posture, I noticed.

"Those policemen are looking for Grace," she whispered with round eyes. "The police know she threatened Gail in the past and want to question her about it. It's true, I heard her say such things many times. Caroline heard it, too. Lots of people have. Grace always accused Gail of drugging the dogs and threatened to give Gail a taste of her own medicine. Now, she can't be found. She's missing. I heard them say she wasn't at her school today. She called in sick and disappeared. Who knows where she's hiding?" Isabella tutted before she left.

Good grief! Were those dog treats really coated with drugs? Could Grace have mixed the treats in dough and made something for Mrs. Bennet to eat? Those white, foam-crusted lips popped into my head. How many cookies would a person need to consume to get to that state? If those dog treats were coated with something I gave Gail in the pharmacy, would that make me an accomplice? Is that why I was a suspect? *Elizabeth Lavenza*, that doesn't even sound like a normal name! I should have known right away! I should have insisted on an identification check, even though Doctor King was very good friends with *Jane Bennet* and knew she was on the up and up.

I felt angry at myself. I invited Grace into my home and went to that place on the river with her. I enjoyed her company and wanted her as a friend. *Rule breakers and deadbeats*, what type of people had I gotten myself involved with? *Stop right there, do not let the rumor mill cloud your mind.*

As the police officers made their way toward the gate, I called to Henry and moved to head them off. Officer Shane Bane could see I wanted to meet them. He gravitated toward me as I leashed Henry. He gave me another neutral smile and bent down to pet Henry. Officer Bane's light brown hair was cut very neat and trimmed with a razor-sharp edge.

"Did you remember something? Should I alert Detective Allen?" he asked.

I shook my head. "Do they know what Mrs. Bennet was poisoned with? Can you tell me what it was?"

He shook his head but his eyes were kind. "I can't say. It's an investigation."

"Is Grace the suspect now? Am I still a suspect?"

"Everyone is a suspect right now." He gave me the detective's answer. *Ugh*, he was so strait-laced. Annoying, but admirable.

Henry and I decided to watch a Netflix show Matt recommended. We each ate a simple dinner, Henry munched on crunchy dog food and I nibbled a grilled cheese sandwich. We turned on a comedy series that was guaranteed to have us laughing uncontrollably, but I wasn't paying attention. All I could think about was Mrs. Bennet's cold and dead face.

Doctor King sent a runner to get the undelivered meds and also called to check up on me. Our pharmacy was in big trouble for supplying Jane Bennet. But how could we be faulted? All those prescriptions had been in the system. Either that old woman was a world-class computer hacker, or someone had helped her. Either way, Doctor King advised me to keep the scope of our pharmacy debacle to myself, even with the police. We needed a lawyer present for those questions, and they needed a warrant. Most of our regular drug traffic was being diverted to another CSV, and our window was closed until further notice. Not to worry, we were on leave with pay. Doctor King sounded harried as he asked about my well-being.

"I feel terrible about all this," I said into the phone.

"Believe me, it's not your fault." Doctor King said. "Those names! That woman was laughing at us. *At me.* For years. You're fine. You caught it. You did well. But keep things on the down low, hushed. Of course, cooperate with the death investigation, but if the police questions get too invasive regarding CSV, please call me so we can get the right representation present." He sounded defeated. "You should stay home and try not to worry about a thing. This infraction shouldn't touch you. You only just started with us, and the Jane Bennet med-runs have been going on for over a year. The murder investigation supersedes the drug investigation, but it looks like the police believe they might be related and have been in and out of here constantly. Let me field the questions about any med-runs other than the *Eleanor Vance* one you unmasked. That way we can avoid any confidentiality issues."

"Doctor King, I think I'm a suspect."

"Nonsense," he said. "They tell everyone they're a suspect. I'm a suspect. I spent three hours at the police station earlier today, telling them everything I know about Jane Bennet. *Gail Bennet.* They pressed me on how I felt when you reported her dubious behavior yesterday. I told them I was furious! What else would I be? But I hadn't logged anything in yet or reported it, and they all but accused me of wanting to hide the mistake. What do they think, I work with lightning speed? And they requested my alibi for yesterday afternoon. *An alibi!* I was dispensing drugs all afternoon! Everyone knows that." His voice was furious.

Not Doctor King, too. Why did they really pull him in for three hours? He could not have done anything to Gail

Bennet after I called him. No more than a couple of hours at most had passed between my phone call to Doctor King and me walking across Gail Bennet's threshold. I glanced at Henry and found him staring at me. We both were not doing a good job watching the television show, so I decided to finish reading that romance novel instead. Just when I got to a heart pounding part in the book, a soft knocking echoed off the door.

Matt needed a work break and had jogged over to see me. He looked disheveled with a slightly unbuttoned shirt and looked exactly like the image of the duke on the cover of that steamy book I slipped under a couch cushion. I invited him in, but he claimed he couldn't stay long. He pulled me against his chest and kissed me. A perfect diversion, kissing was a much better distraction than watching television or reading a book. One of his large hands when into my hair, holding my head under my ear, and the other went to the small of my back, warm and strong. I was overcome with a flooding rush of heat. His kisses turned deep, and I shamelessly ran my hands over all his nice muscles. He paused and whispered,

"Is this okay?"

"Yes," I managed before sinking my teeth onto his neck.

I really was a vampire! I could barely contain myself at the feel of his sternocleidomastoid under my lips. I followed that angled muscle up to his ear. His ear! As I nibbled on his lope, we dropped onto the couch. His hands moved to my hips, then traveled upward until I felt the heat of his wrists touching the sides of my breasts. His lips roved all over my neck and collar area, then down to test the limits of my scoop neck shirt. I felt him brush aside my teardrop gemstone with his nose. The smell of him was earthy and intoxicating. I reached down and slipped my hand under the hem of his T-shirt and just about fainted at the feel of tight rippling abdominal muscles under my fingertips. We wrestled a little longer until it became apparent that a rather large dog head was attempting to squeeze in between us. We separated, laughing at Henry and his interference.

Matt stared at me with his golden tiger's eyes and a closed-mouth grin. I glanced at Henry, the voice of reason. I wasn't sure what I would have done if Henry had not stuck his nose in there. Behavior like this, with a man I hadn't known for a full week, was unusual for me. I wondered what he would do if I asked him back to my bedroom? Would he accept?

"Would you like some coffee?" I asked instead. He nodded.

We moved to the kitchen and I poured two cups of coffee.

We sat staring across the table quietly with Henry as a chaperone. He followed us into the kitchen and lay on the ground right between us, keeping an eye on us, acting as my own personal Charlotte Bartlett. Matt eyed Henry and chuckled.

"I'm glad he's behaving," Matt said, "And looking out for you. I'm sorry if I got carried away in there. It's been a crazy week, and I'm not acting very steady."

I shook my head. "You're acting fine."

Matt's tiger eyes changed to a darker shade. "I wonder why they keep saying it was a suspicious death. What was so suspicious about it? Are you worried that they called you a suspect?"

I shrugged my shoulders.

"Why wouldn't they assume it was a simple heart attack, like with Joe? She was very out of shape. Unhealthy. No one called Joe's death suspicious."

"It was definitely poisoning, even if they won't say it. She had dried foam coming out her nostrils and mouth. It looked suspicious."

That made him appear ill. I lowered my voice to almost a whisper.

"Do you know Grace well? Do you think she could have done something with those dog treats I gave her? Isabella believes Grace was capable of it, especially as she's gone missing. What do you think? Maybe she didn't intend for anyone to die, it could have been an accident, a prank gone wrong."

He sat up straighter, happier. "You're right! You gave her those dog treats, and she talked about baking something nasty for Mrs. Bennet, she always talked about it. You're absolutely right. I bet Grace baked something and gave it to Mrs. Bennet."

Why did he look so happy? Was he relieved that there was a more likely suspect than me? Had he actually believed I could have killed Gail Bennet? My feelings were suddenly hurt. I sat in silence as he ran through what Grace must have done. Either added the treats to cookie dough or recovered as much of the powder as she could. No, Grace would have made scones, he mused. Grace had baked scones for the dog park folks before, and Mrs. Bennet had raved about the lemon-flavored ones. Matt always thought Grace was just talking, joking in her dark sarcastic way, but who knew what a person was capable of. No wonder she went missing.

"I saw pastries in the living room. Right next to the spilled tea," I said, staring at his golden-brown eyes. "Did you think it could have been me at first?"

"No! No," he said earnestly and grabbed my hand. "I didn't understand why they considered you a suspect, you barely knew Gail Bennet. No, I never thought you could be involved." He stood and pulled me up for another embrace. He whispered in my ear, "I'm sorry I've been acting so strange, it was hard losing Joe. Then, this thing with Mrs.

Bennet. Could someone from our park have killed her, like Grace? Or… There were definitely people that hated her." He turned worried eyes on me. "Just be careful, okay? Don't trust anyone."

Then, he left, as he had to get back to work. But I was more confused than ever. Be careful? Of who, of what? I looked at Henry.

"If it was Grace," I told Henry, "then it was a terrible joke gone wrong. Why would that turn her into a mass murderer? Why should I be afraid of Grace?"

*Oh, you innocent girl,* Henry's wise eyes seemed to say, *who knew Grace got hold of those doggy treats? If she wanted to cover up her terrible blunder, she would need to make sure anyone who knew about the treats stayed quiet.* But would Grace go so far as to kill me? I imagined that instead of multiple homicides, she'd show up begging me not to tell about the treats. I crossed over to Henry and stroked his head.

"I am so glad you are going to be here tonight," I told him. "I am so glad I didn't let that terrible Troy guy take you away."

Henry's tail just thumped. After another episode of our television show, we went off to bed, and I kept my fingers crossed that I made the right decision about keeping Henry with me. I decided to finish reading that fascinating novel about Maggie and the duke before falling asleep. Those two characters were destined for a dramatic, climatic end, and I desperately wanted to reach a climatic end to something before falling asleep.

# Day Eight

## with Henry

I was not sure why Henry had turned into a different dog, but I was just glad he did. The next morning, we celebrated another night of no mischief. I ruminated on what I might finally be doing right and concluded that we just needed time to get used to one another. Or maybe he liked that I was needy. I turned to Henry with suspicious eyes.

"What were you thinking those first few days?"

There were more messages from the CSV and Doctor King. The police wanted access to the CSV system and pulled him in for questioning again. He reminded me to let him know if they pulled me in, so he could get a representative to go with me. *I wonder why I have not been pulled into the station for questioning yet.* Maybe I wasn't much of a suspect. Or maybe they were saving the best suspect for last.

Henry and I did yoga in the living room again. I didn't say it to him, but my crouching dog pose was much better than his crouching dog pose. Henry was not stretching to his limit. But it was nice to have a partner, and Henry was very funny. Afterward, we sat silently, and I watched the dog park's morning crowd slowly trickle in. People were talking about the suspicious death investigation again. I could tell by their body language and by the one woman who kept glancing at my house. I had an urge to go online and check out the neighborhood app, to discover what people were saying.

Then, I spotted Grace. She jogged right past the dog park without Mollie. She headed right for my front door!

Oh my God! What should I do? What should I say? What could she want? I hopped off the sofa, and the next thing I knew, my bell rang. Should I call Officer Bane? Detective Allen? Matt? What do you do when a suspected poisoner rings your doorbell?

I answered the door.

"Sarah." Grace seemed a little surprised I opened the door so quickly. "Sarah, you look okay."

"I am okay," I said. "How are you?"

"It's just. I was worried. The other night you didn't answer the door. We knocked and knocked and knew you were in here, but you never answered. That cop told us to leave you alone."

"I think I was in shock," I said.

Grace shifted from foot to foot. "That's understandable. I can hardly believe it myself. It must have been terrible finding her. They say the dog…" Grace shook her head. "I'm glad you answered the door."

"Did you know the police were looking for you?"

Grace rolled her eyes. "I know. They found me late last night when I got home. I had been at… a friend's house." Grace took a step forward. "They're questioning everyone about Gail Bennet and said everyone's a suspect. The police were interested in knowing about the doggie treats I had. Did *you* tell them about the doggie treats?"

I stared at her.

"It's no problem if you did, but I can't help being upset that you would think I could… Whoever told the police I got hold of those treats insisted I used them to poison Gail Bennet. That's why I had to go to the station for questioning."

"I didn't tell them," I said. "No one asked me anything about the treats."

Curious eyes from the dog park were spying on us and I waved Grace inside. Grace did not seem like the type of person to poison Gail Bennet. Plus, the cat was already out of the bag when it came to the doggy treats. There was no reason for her to murder me now. Plus, she was a schoolteacher. Teachers might be sarcastic and critical about handwriting, but I doubted they went around poisoning people. Grace embraced me as she entered and patted Henry on the head before following me into the kitchen. Grace would rather have tea than coffee, and we each ended up with a cup of Earl Grey Black with honey.

"Four different people told the cops I threatened to feed Gail Bennet a concoction of her own medicine and said they believed I would do it. One of those people knew I got hold of some of her treats the other day..." Grace rolled her eyes nervously. "I guess dry humor is not a big thing these days."

I stirred my tea.

"I admit, somewhere deep inside, I hoped karma would strike her. But I wasn't hoping she would die from it! I guess she was poisoned with something, the police seemed pretty certain of that. Do you think an autopsy told them it was a poisoning? This fast?"

"Mrs. Bennet had froth on her lips and nostrils, a sure sign of poisoning or drug overdose."

Grace let out a long breath. She tucked a hand under her sharp chin. I suddenly wondered if Matt told the authorities about those treats. Did he call the police right after he left my house? Was he worried about Grace and those doggie treats?

"I took another sick day because I couldn't imagine going into work after that interrogation. I was there until two in the morning. And I wanted to see you today. When you didn't answer the door, I was worried." Her gaze was sharp, taking me in. "Just so you know, I did not poison Mrs. Bennet with her own doggie treats, or with anything else. The police confiscated the dog treats when they dropped me off this morning. I think they're going to ask you about them. Like how many treats are supposed to be in the bag," she said.

"How many treats *are* supposed to be in the bag?" I looked down at my tea, worried that I didn't truly know this woman on the other side of my table.

"That's the thing," Grace said softly, and I met her eyes. She was upset. "I threw them out. All but two of them. I vacuum sealed those two in plastic and put them in an envelope to express mail them to Quest, a lab that tests for chemicals, toxins, and other things. They said they only needed two, so I threw the rest away. Inconvenient for me that the garbage was picked up yesterday morning."

She stared right into my eyes. Would a liar be able to do that?

"Look, I hated that woman," she said. "But I did not poison her. And I feel guilty for hating her like this. I feel like my hate made her die, so I now feel very guilty that she's dead. And it upsets me to think people believe I would do something so hateful. I know I look guilty, and with my luck, it'll turn out she died of whatever is on those dog treats, and now I can only account for two of them. This is fucked up."

"It is. It's very unfortunate. I'm just glad you showed up again," I said softly.

"Do you think I'm the prime suspect?" she asked.

"I don't know," I said. "It was upsetting when nobody could find you. I admit it, I didn't know what to think when you went missing. It felt… odd. I admit to speculating about why you mysteriously disappeared. Where did you go?"

"It's nobody's business." Grace's sharp chin jutted out. Then, she softened and spoke in a low conspiratorial manner. "I was with a friend, a friend with benefits. It was a strange two days, and I needed a diversion. I never imagined playing hooky to meet a man would make me the prime suspect in a murder investigation."

*A friend with benefits.* Did people actually have those? I wondered briefly if Matt had ever been Grace's friend with benefits. I didn't think so. But obviously, George had been, at least once, that was what Matt implied. Why hadn't I ever had a friend with benefits? I understood kissing as a diversion, as it had worked the previous night for me. I definitely felt ready for a friend with benefits, irresistible and passionate benefits hopefully. My heart rate pumped up a notch thinking about it. Good grief, that romance novel mixed with an idle mind and summer hormones made for a powerful stimulating love potion.

Not long after Grace left, the doorbell rang again. A man in a green baseball cap and purple shirt stood outside and I could see his small white truck on the curb, the handyman. He appeared a tad bit confused because most of the folks in the dog park stood staring at him. My front stoop had become a popular visual attraction lately. I invited him inside and led him through the kitchen to show him the broken screen door. I offered him coffee. He wore baggy old jeans and a Sacramento King's T-shirt. He forgot to take off his hat, and he blew on his tepid coffee before every sip.

"I could bend it back into shape and rescreen it, but the latch is cracked and might give you problems. It looks like a standard size. I could swing by Home Depot and pick up a new door and install it. I think you'd be much happier with a new one."

"Would it be too much trouble to put in a doggy door?"

"Not at all. I can do that easily. I can get the parts from Home Depot. It slides right into the door frame." He took out his measuring tape and wrote down numbers on his hand with a black pen.

"Would you like a piece of paper?"

He laughed. "No, no, it's a standard size." He looked into the living room at Henry. "Better get the large door for that guy. Do you want a basic door? There's a fancy one you can control with a smartphone."

"We're basic around here," I told him. Then, I showed him the bathroom doorknob and towel bar, and he laughed.

My house turned out to be a busy crossroads that morning. As the repairman left to shop at Home Depot, the Wilson couple stopped by with a loaf of homemade raisin bread. They wanted to check on me. Then, other folks stopped by, people who had been in my house the day we found Joe, but I didn't invite anyone else in. Most folks inquired if I needed anything and probably thought I was taking a few sick days due to the stress of finding Mrs. Bennet's dead body. Nobody knew about the pharmacy shut down. I spotted a police cruiser for the second time that morning and noticed Officer Shane Bane in the driver's seat, cool and handsome. He waved as he drove past, a neutral expression on his face. He wore a fat black watch on his wrist, old fashioned. His partner was not with him. For a moment, I recalled his neck and the scent he gave off, a pleasant calming aroma. I felt like I let him down in some way, which was ridiculous because I'd only met him twice. *Did he see me as a murderess or an accomplice?* I wondered when that detective would drop in and ask me how many treats were in the bag. Then, I got a call from an unknown number.

"Hello?"

"Sarah! Hi, it's me, Josh."

"Oh, Josh. Hi. How's your trip going?"

Henry lifted his head. Did he know I was speaking to Josh? Or maybe he knew Josh's name? Henry actually stood up, shifted around, and sat back down facing away. Looks like someone felt very upset at Josh.

"Busy. You know how these conventions go. I can't understand half of what people are saying out here. And these people drink all night. It's harrowing."

"It sounds harrowing," I said.

"Troy said you refused to let him take Henry. Is that right?"

"He wanted to put Henry in a crate," I said.

Henry glanced over his shoulder with sorrowful eyes.

"That's not unusual, especially if Henry was acting up. Lots of people keep a dog in a crate. It's not like a wooden box; a dog crate is like a wire cage. He'd be able to see out of it. Also, there's another guy in the office, Stan. Henry always behaves for Stan. Stan gets back tomorrow, and Troy can pass him off right away, no problem."

"I'm not letting anyone put Henry in a crate. I'll keep Henry with me."

Oh my, look at that tail thump! That made me smile.

"Are you sure?"

"I'm sure." I winked at Henry.

"Okay, but I'm going to give Stan your number, just in case. Maybe he can give you tips on Henry if you have any more problems. Or he can fetch him. Stan won't put him in a crate, I promise you that."

"Don't worry about Henry, we're fine," I told him.

"Have I said this before? You're a fantastic woman, Sarah. I can't wait to see you. Just three more days! You are going to love what I bring you."

"Josh, don't bring me anything," I said. "I need to clarify something about us."

"Don't say it," Josh cut me off. "Just wait until I get there before you say anything or decide anything. I can fix this."

I didn't see how. After the crazy physical stirrings Matt inspired, I realized there wasn't a possibility Josh could be my summer romance. Yes, Josh had several nice check marks on my list for an appropriate partner, but Josh lacked the most important check, the passion check.

By the time the repairman returned to insert a doggie door and repair the bathroom, I was worried about Matt. He hadn't answered his phone all morning, and I wondered why. I became anxious. There was a killer out there, and Matt wasn't answering his phone. I didn't even know where he lived. How could I check on him?

Henry and I escaped into the dog park to get out of the house and hear the gossip. Isabella perched in her typical spot and glanced up, but her facial expression remained cautiously aloof. She tilted her head at me but turned her eyes back to the dogs without a verbal greeting. I sat down and stared at Isabella until she looked at me.

"So, what is the gossip now?" I asked.

Isabella eyed me with a hard, accusing stare.

"People don't know you," she said. "The police are always driving by your house. Look, there they are again." We watched Officer Shane Bane cruise past, surveying us with a neutral expression. "It's strange, you show up and suddenly two people are dead. There's a rumor that you're running away from something, or someone. I know some of it is just silly talk, but it makes me wonder. I don't know what to believe. And now, people who have been around you are being questioned by the police, at the police station!" She shrugged and moved the dark bang out of her eyes. "I don't want to be questioned at the police station or be mixed up in whatever is happening here."

Good grief, did the entire neighborhood believe I went around killing people?

"Who's being questioned?"

"You know, everyone. Caroline, George." She pointed to a man on the far end of the dog run. "Antonio said they are searching Lola's house right now. You know, Matt's sister's house, because he's staying there. She isn't even here, and they're searching her house."

So, that's why Matt wasn't answering his phone.

"What do they think they'll find?" I asked.

"I don't know? The murder weapon."

"The murder weapon? I thought Mrs. Bennet was poisoned."

"That's not the latest information." Isabella leaned forward and narrowed her eyes. "They say she had a single gunshot wound to her temple. Just one. And so did Joe. Execution style."

"Who said this? Where is this information coming from? The police?"

Isabella shook her head. "The police aren't saying anything, they're covering things up. They're trying to pin it on that little boy, Micah. They want to wrap it all up and blame him. But they need to find the right gun, the murder weapon. I'm not sure what exactly you're mixed up in, but leave me out of it." Isabella suddenly stood and moved to the opposite side of the park.

Good grief, the gossip mill had gone off the deep end. Then, I saw him. Matt rushed into the park with his two jumpy dogs. He scanned the enclosure before he came clanging through the gate. He threw two tennis balls for his dogs, then rushed over. He slid onto the bench beside me.

"The police are at my house, so I've got to get back soon. I told them I was taking the dogs for a quick walk. They're searching everywhere, and they won't tell me what they're looking for." He ran a hand through his messy hair, worried. "But we're all thinking about getting together to share what we know. Just our small group. Grace, Caroline, George, and Bob, and anyone else who's been pulled in for questioning and told not to leave the area. Everyone asked if you would like to come, too."

"Does everyone want to want to meet at my house again?"

Matt shook his head.

"Bob's house. That squad car keeps cruising past your place, and we aren't hiding, but we're not flaunting, either. We're calling it a swim party, so wear a swimsuit. Bob's on the opposite end of Crossbridge Drive, on the right. You can cut through the park to get there." Then, he kissed me in front of the entire dog park before taking Bluebell and Stella back home. I turned to see Isabella staring at me through narrow, judging eyes.

I might be the prime suspect in a suspicious death investigation, and also culpable in a legal investigation at my place of employment, and at the very least, the topic of malicious neighborhood gossip, but the thing I found myself manically stressing about was which swimsuit to wear. I feared coming across as an east coast prude with my full coverage one-piece, but my larger two-piece happened to be an eye-catching red with very sheer material not meant to get wet, and the smaller bikini was scandalously small. Grace would definitely wear something cute, and with all her pushups and jumping jacks she possessed the body to pull it off. I looked at Henry.

"Well, we do yoga. And yoga makes for a nice bikini body, too, right, Henry?"

Henry didn't say anything, but I knew he agreed. He padded around and plopped his head on the scandalously small swimsuit. Good grief, was that the one? There was a sudden sharp knock on my front door. Detective Allen stood on the stoop. He wore a different shirt and tie but sported the same patched sleeve corded jacket. I invited him inside, and we sat on the sofa gazing out at the dog park.

"Good day, Doctor Fitzgerald." Detective Allan smiled as he pulled out his notepad and thick pen. "Tell me everything you know about Micah. Did he ever go into the pharmacy to see you or Doctor King?"

"Not that I know." That was a confusing question. "As I said before, I only met him once, in the dog park. I understand he did odd jobs for Mrs. Bennet. I've seen him walking her dog."

He nodded.

"Officer Bane reported that Grace Briar paid you a visit this morning." His eyes were watchful. "Can you tell me what she wanted?"

"She dropped in the say hello. To see how I was doing," I said. "And to ask if I told you about the doggy treats Mrs. Bennet gave me. There were about seven treats in the bag, I think."

"Did she know about the false name Mrs. Bennet used at the pharmacy? Did she know anything about Mrs. Bennet's med-runs?"

"I can't say," I said. "If she did, she certainly never mentioned it to me."

"I take it you're aware the police searched Matthew Diller's residence today," he said. "Do you have any idea what we were looking for?"

"No, what were you looking for?"

"Drugs." He watched me. "Possible prescription drugs Mrs. Bennet may have picked up."

"You told me that pretty easily," I observed. "I wonder why."

"Are you aware your boyfriend visited Mrs. Bennet the day she died?"

"You mean Matt Diller," I asked. I certainly wasn't aware of that. "He wanted to speak with her about Joe. The old man that died earlier this week after his dog was put down. If you're looking for drugs…" I wasn't sure how to tell them about George. "I think that man, George Johnson, may have gotten drugs from her."

He jotted something into his book. Then, the detective asked me to recap the exact time I called Doctor King and the tone of his voice when I relayed my suspicions about the false prescription. Could I remember his exact words? Did I tell anyone else? What time did I leave for Mrs. Bennet's house? Which route did I take? Do I recall seeing anyone else on the street? Who, where, what were they doing? Any strange cars driving by? What did I see in her living room, the kitchen, the hall, and her bedroom? After hashing through it all again, he finally thanked me and left, still confirming that, yes, everyone was still a suspect.

The homes on the opposite end of Crossbridge Drive were slightly larger than those on my end of the street. The sidewalks grew wider, and the driveways morphed from smooth concrete to aggregated pebbles. The front door steps gained porches and even the cars changed shape. Instead of bulky SUVs mixed with small, dented economy vehicles lining the curbs, large sedans and electric vehicles were parked in each driveway. Bob's wife, Joanne, answered the door, and she led me through her living room to the backyard and the pool. I noticed they collected a mixture of different stringed instruments in their living room, mandolins, guitars, and even a blonde acoustic double bass.

Bob stood under the shady awning on his large back patio pouring small shots of whisky for everyone. They were already having a nice, roaring, party. I declined a shot of what Bob called the "best single malt ever" and accepted the pool safe cup of wine instead. I noticed George, Matt, Caroline, and Grace had already been in the water because everyone wore a damp swimsuit and had wet hair. I couldn't help staring at Matt, transfixed. He bulged all muscles, with a nicely shaped torso. I couldn't believe such a fantastically structured man was interested in me.

He stepped near and kissed me on the cheek, establishing our new status as friends with kissing benefits. Then, I noticed his back and the nice diamond shape his rhomboids made on that smooth canvas, yet his flank area appeared scarred over. It healed long ago, but his skin was a wavy discolored expanse. Everyone quieted for a moment and I felt bad for drawing attention to his scars.

"Pearl Hill fire, up in Washington State. It got a few of us," he said stoically and the talking resumed.

Everyone migrated to the cool water with drinks in hand. Two large queen palm trees and colorful flowers decorated the small backyard. A wooden barrel-shaped steam sauna sat right off the patio, and the Battens collected gnome and mermaid statues which were scattered along the fence. The pool dwarfed the backyard and was outlined with tumbled quartzite stones instead of regular brick or cement coping. A cutout section in the pool bubbled and steamed, and in the opposite corner, a small waterfall trickled over large stones creating a tinkling melody.

Joanne handed me a pool towel with a graphic image of Snoopy and Woodstock hugging. Every pool towel hanging on chair backs were cartoon images of the Peanuts gang, and Joanne shrugged

"I would blame it on my kids," she explained, "but I love Snoopy. Don't laugh at my pool plates later. Peanuts is my pool area theme."

Those images brought back fond memories of my father and listening to him chuckle at vintage cartoons and comic strips. When I was very young, he helped me cut out the *Peanuts* comic strip from the newspaper, and we put together quite a scrapbook with those clippings, using rubber cement and colorful pens. It was his way of spending time with me, making that book, and then reading the cartoon panels to each other late at night. I smiled at Joanne.

"I love Snoopy, too." I accepted the offered towel.

Caroline wore a classy pearl and pink one-piece swimsuit and slipped into the bubbling hot tub instead of the cool pool, and all the guys wore long surfer shorts. Joanne wondered aloud if meeting and talking during a murder investigation was okay.

"No one said we couldn't talk," Grace said. Thank goodness, Grace wore an extremely cute bikini, even smaller than the suit Henry picked out for me. She dove right into the deep end, barely making a splash, and glided underwater to the shallow end of the pool. Grace wasn't shy, so I wouldn't be shy, either.

I dropped my things on a lounge chair, towel, keys, phone, while Matt ferried my wine cup to the pool and started down the steps into the water toward George and

Bob. I was a little miffed George chose to stare at me as I shimmied out of my sundress. *How rude.* I acted like I didn't notice his glaring inspection as I followed Matt into the water, but Matt noticed it. He spun around to look at me, eyes widening at my bikini.

"Wow," he sputtered. "You look nice. That's a very nice swimsuit."

Good grief, his tone of voice set my heart pounding. He passed me my drink and gravitated closer with his now free hand claiming my waist. I felt his fingertips pass over the skin along my hip and then stay there, resting, fire under the water. Grace splashed up and suggested a game of beach ball volleyball. We didn't have a net, so we passed the ball around while Joanne and Caroline watched from the hot tub. Then, we retreated to the shady side of the pool and gathered around the curve of the hot tub. Bob told us all about some sort of musical chord progression chart he created. After a bit, someone mentioned the two policemen who were hanging out in the neighborhood, and everyone chatted about Officer Shane Bane and his partner Glen. I noticed Joanne was a little hard of hearing and needed things repeated every so often.

"Who wants to go first?" Grace suddenly blurted. Nobody answered. "Okay, I will. The police asked me a ton of questions about drugs and wanted to know if I have been buying illegal pills from Gail Bennet. They actually asked me if I heard the name Sibyl Vane before." Grace was laughing now. "I thought they were trying to mess with my mind."

"Who's Sibyl Vane?" Joanne asked.

Grace told her. "The love interest of *Dorian Gray*, you know, the actress he ruined by being such an ass bastard. My goodness, I'm an English teacher, so of course, I know Sibyl Vane. Apparently, Gail Bennet adopted a couple of names from novels to get her drugs from CSV, like Eleanor Vance and Sibyl Vane and Jane Bennet." Grace stared at me. "They say you were duped and filled some of her orders. They asked if I thought you might harm her because of it, or if I thought you'd want to get the evidence back. The police said you could lose your license."

Everyone stared at me.

"I wanted to confront her, not kill her. The pharmacy has been filling her mock orders for a long time. Yes, it's going to have some major repercussions for someone at CSV, but her prescriptions were all in the system. Nobody should lose their license over it." At least, I didn't think so. How could we be liable for falsified records in the system?

"I figured something like that," Grace said.

"Maybe Doctor King helped her," Caroline said softly. "He's the one who's been there all along, filling the prescriptions. I know, I used to work there, and I've seen his temper. He hardly ever loses it, but a couple of years ago, after his divorce, he was always angry. And he's always been chummy with Mrs. Bennet. Do you think Doctor King lost his temper because she fooled him and went to her house and…"

"No!" I interjected. Was that possible? No, not old Doctor King. Caroline's accusation seemed like a very long stretch of the imagination. But the police did pull him in twice for questioning. I began to rerun every encounter I'd ever had with Doctor King, and every one of them shouted harmless, old, grandpa type.

"Look, I'm pretty street smart and can tell you exactly what's going on here," Bob leaned on the spa wall. "She stepped on the toes of some shady people, that's what. There's a gang running this area, drug dealers from south Natomas are my guess. I bet her death is a drug-related war killing, a hit. Gail Bennet overstepped her boundaries with her pill peddling and was taken out, simple as that. And that boy Micah, I wouldn't be surprised if he worked for them. Played both sides of the street, maybe he had to pick a side. He was a sly boy. I've seen that boy with shady people. Very shady."

"Oh, please, you're so street smart," Joanne teased him. "Wouldn't a simple overdose be the most likely story? They say she had a ton of drugs in her house, and it makes more sense than a murder. I don't know why the police refuse to come out and just say it. They're causing a terrible load of gossip by being so closed-lipped."

"Isabella said something about a gunshot wound to the temple," I said softly.

Bob laughed. "Yes, and down the street, they're saying it was an icepick to the neck. People love making things up on that neighborhood app. No, it was a definite poisoning from everything the detective said. In my questioning session, the police talked about the drugs at her house, in her sugar bowl, in the candy jars. They even found drugs in her teapot. I think she was meeting people, shady people, and she made a tea to drug them. I think someone figured it out, and forced her to drink her own tea or something along those lines."

"Or she accidentally overdosed on her tea and tainted treats," his wife insisted.

The Battens each rose from the water at the same time. Joanne traipsed off to check on the food and prepare a salad, and Bob announced his plan to blend up some margaritas. They insisted the rest of us relax and enjoy the pool, more refreshments were on the way.

"The police must not believe she would overdose all on her own," George said. "Come on, Grace, admit it. Did you make scones with those doggy treats? I know you got hold of some. Nobody around here would tell on you. We all know it was an accident."

"I did not make scones or anything else with those treats," Grace hissed. "And by the way, somebody did try to tell on me, George. Someone informed the police that I acquired some of her doggie treats, and they believed I feed them to Gail Bennet in the form of a scone." Grace spun to face Matt. "Did you tell them that? If I recall, you were sitting right there when Sarah gave them to me. So, you or Sarah must have said something to the police and Sarah already assured me it wasn't her."

"No!" Matt defended himself.

"Oh, relax," George said. "Everyone watched you take those treats the other day. Everyone watched Mrs. Bennet passed them to Sarah before leaving and then watched her give them to you. The dogs only line up and sit at attention for Gail Bennet's treats. And no, I didn't rat you out about it."

Grace seemed to accept his explanation but still gave Matt the eye.

"She did have pastries on her coffee table," Matt said softly, defiantly. "Cookies, brownies, and *scones*."

Grace shot a look at Caroline, and Caroline flinched. Caroline shook her head.

"You always bake brownies for Mrs. Bennet's tea," Grace said to her. "For as long as I've known you."

Caroline didn't answer.

"This time, did you perhaps bake some of your husband's special brownies and share a few with Mrs. Bennet?" Grace asked again.

George and Matt both gawked at Caroline, just as confused as I felt.

"I baked a few brownies, but I certainly didn't poison them," Caroline snapped.

Grace's eyes softened. "Maybe it was an accident, Caroline, like George said. Just tell us. Were they the special brownies?"

"It wasn't an accident." Caroline immediately rose from the hot tub, warm water splashing everywhere. "You're trying to divert the blame, Grace. I saw lemon scones on her coffee table when I went over there, and we all know how you've talked about it in the past. And the special brownies I make for my husband wouldn't kill anyone. They're just a sleep aid."

"I was just joking," Grace said. "Where are you going?"

Caroline left in a huff. She slipped into a pretty orange and yellow sundress and gathered up her large bag. She waved to all of us in the water with a scowl on her face and went into the house, still a little damp. Joanne followed her into the house, and I watched them pause in the living room to chat for a little while.

"What just happened?" George asked. "Is that suspicious or what?"

"She makes special brownies for her husband. You know what an ass bastard Eric is. Did you see her eye?" Grace told us in a hushed tone. "She told me months ago that she adds some of her sleeping pills into the mix so she can get a quiet night. But I think she may have gone a little overboard this time and passed those brownies to Mrs. Bennet. Could sleeping pills in brownies have killed Mrs. Bennet? Would that be enough to poison a person?"

"Spiked brownies or spiked scones or maybe both mixed with the tea." George grinned.

Grace glared at him.

"What is your opinion, doctor?" George didn't look at me when he asked. He stared into his drink instead. Was he finally trying to be polite? "Could eating a brownie made with sleeping pills or scones made with... whatever she gives those dogs cause her to overdose like that?"

That was a good question. Just how spiked did the brownies or scones need to be? Had she been on any medication already? I remembered the mountain of foam on her mouth, and I remembered the mountain of *suvorexant* Caroline picked up with her brownie mix.

"She would need to eat a lot of brownies, I think, to get to death. Of course, it depends on how toxic they were and if she had something else in her system, like from the tea." I recalled the living room with all the photographs and that fancy tea set on the coffee table. *One cup was overturned.* "I think the tea is more suspicious and would be more to blame. It would be much easier to drink a toxic amount than to eat a bunch of pastries. That would be my guess, especially after what Bob said about them finding drugs in the teapot."

"Maybe Micah did it then," Grace said softly. "Mrs. Bennet bragged about how he often helped her get ready for her weekly tea parties. Maybe he spiked her tea."

Matt nodded stiffly at Grace's new theory. Their silent agreement diffused the nervous energy that had built up. Bob brought out a tray full of slushy drinks to offer as he settled into the hot tub. He said Caroline needed to run home to make dinner for her husband.

Everyone relayed tales of the police interrogation. The police questioned Matt about his background and why he had gone to see Mrs. Bennet. They pressed him on details of his visit, how long was he there, what did he do? *He just talked about Joe.* The police asked George if he had known the scope of Mrs. Bennet's drug business. *He didn't, but guessed it was not small.* The police asked George for an alibi for that afternoon, but he had been out biking all day and didn't visit Mrs. Bennet. The police questioned Bob about the dog complaints and how he felt about them. *He couldn't care less.* The police asked each of them what they knew about me. *Nice*, Matt had said. *Reserved*, Grace told them. *Pleasant and polite*, Bob reported.

"I told them you were beautiful and sexy." George grinned, and his bright eyes fell on me, all of me. I became suddenly anxious remembering his strong grip and minor assault. "And that you had an out-of-town boyfriend." He glanced at Matt.

*Ugh!* Luckily, Joanne called us over to their glass-topped picnic table where there was an offer of food. I noticed both Matt and Grace gave George the evil eye as we moved under the shady awning. George smiled pleasantly at them and joked loudly with Bob about something to do with sports. I sat as far away from George as possible. Right after eating and cleaning up, Grace decided to leave, and Joanne walked her to the door. Bob urged Matt into the house to show off the guitars and his hundred year-old mandolin, leaving me alone with George on the back patio, drinking a thick Margarita. I noticed my key ring in George's hand.

"Hey, what are you doing with those?"

His face appeared shocked, and he opened his hand as if he didn't realize he was holding my keys. He put them on the table between us, embarrassed.

"They were on the ground," he said. "I just picked them up and was fiddling with them. I was going to give them to Bob. I'm a little nervous and needed to fiddle with something. I wasn't trying to take them."

I didn't know if I believed him. "Why are you so nervous?" I accused.

"You, you're making me nervous," he said. "I mean, look at you. I'm not kidding, you're beautiful and very sexy in that, that very swimming swimsuit. You went from shy to wow quite suddenly." He flashed his devilish grin. "Your legs are spectacular, doc, you should show them off more. I feel the need to warn you about Matt. He's a washout. He pretends to be the sad and brave fireman, burned by love and fire, but he did something very stupid and got kicked to the curb, by both the girl and the department. He'll never admit it to you, but no one just quits the fire department. He screws things up and runs away. He's not the man for you. You'll get bored with those cute biceps sooner than you think and want a grown-up."

I began gathering my things. "You're despicable."

"Wait, are you going to tell people what I did? I don't want anyone here to know." He glanced up to make sure everyone was occupied inside. "About what I tried to do at the pharmacy, I don't want anyone to know about that. I'm embarrassed about it. That's not me, and I'm ashamed I tried it. I just wanted to up my training regimen, perfectly normal for riders to take a little something to enhance their performance. I'm a dedicated athlete. I'm trying to up my ranking."

"I can't keep secrets from the police," I said.

"You don't have to." His transparent eyes were sad. "The police already know I got pills from Mrs. Bennet. It's the gossip mill I'm worried about. I don't want it to get out, you've heard how people talk around here. I would appreciate it if you kept that information to yourself. In time, you might find I'm not that bad. You might even grow to like me. Women find me very likable, I'm a nice guy."

I grabbed my keys off the table and grabbed my bag. I was done. I could not stay a moment longer, not if George was going to keep staring at my hips. I found Joanne and thanked her for a lovely time, then popped into the living room where Bob and Matt were playing music together. Matt strummed on a nice guitar, and Bob tinkered on a nice mandolin. Matt did not look remotely ready to go anywhere, he seemed involved in a deep conversation with Bob. I wasn't sure if he even noticed when I left, but I needed to get away from everyone to clear my head.

Henry lounged on his chewed-up area rug, sleeping. I wasn't sure if he used his new doggy door, but the house still looked in good order. That pool party unsettled me, and I felt very warm from too much sun, and I had a heavy head. I drank a large glass of water and wished I would have ignored the margaritas after drinking wine because I still felt very intoxicated.

Out in the dog park, the afternoon crowd was in full swing without Matt or Grace or George. The sky already softened to a light orange, and I could see late thunderstorms over the mountains threatening to move into the valley again. Then, I noticed Caroline sitting in the dog park staring right at my window. Actually, she was staring right into my window, right at me. She rose slowly to her feet, dreamily, before suddenly rushing out the gate and crossing the street. She made a beeline to my front door, and I opened it before she could knock.

"I need to talk to you," she looked stricken.

I debated whether I should invite her in, but she didn't give me much choice. She pushed her way into my home and stood just inside the door. Henry opened his eyes and rose to his haunches. Did he sense my anxiety?

"Please hear me out," she begged.

"Look, I don't—"

"I drugged the brownies," she confessed. "I did. But they weren't deadly. I only put in enough of those sleeping pills to put me and Eric to sleep. Just one or two brownies will do it, and I admit taking some to Gail. I only took four brownies to her house. Four. Even if she ate them all in one sitting, that couldn't possibly have killed her, could it?" Caroline burst into tears.

I didn't know what to say. Could she have killed Mrs. Bennet by accident? It was a possibility. It seemed more likely it was the tea, or maybe a combination of the two. Either way, the police should be notified. Micah was a small boy, and it was terrible to think he could be in jail for a crime he didn't fully commit.

"We should call the police," I said softly. "And tell them about those brownies, just in case."

"They already know about the brownies." She peered through tear-stained eyes at me, wiping her face with shaky hands. "I already confessed about them during questioning, and they wrote it all down. But they were so fixated on asking about Gail Bennet the drug dealer and if I knew about the pill peddling. I've been waiting for someone to come and arrest me. Do you think they're waiting for a toxicology report? And I'm scared to death of Eric. I'm positive the police told Eric what I said about the brownies. He disappeared right after the police interview, and I'm afraid to sleep in my own house now. I thought he would be out here, but he's missing."

Matt strolled into view outside, moving toward my door, bright and happy. He looked sun-tanned and fresh, handsome. Before I could say anything, he rapped loudly, and I watched Caroline's paranoid eyes dart around as I moved past her and opened the door. For a moment, everyone exchanged glances, then Caroline and Matt slowly exchanged places as they mumbled greetings to each other. I followed Caroline out onto the front walk.

"Wait," I said.

She stopped and spun around, still teary-eyed.

"I meant what I said in CSV the other day," I told her. "My door is always open."

"You mean I can stay here tonight?"

I nodded. "If you want to, I have a spare room."

"Thank you, I'll go and get a few things before the rain sets in. Thank you."

Matt observed the entire exchange with an odd expression on his face. He closed the door hard and turned to me.

"What was that about? What did she say?"

"She's afraid of her husband and needs a place to stay," I said.

"It sounds like *he* should be afraid of *her*." Matt watched Caroline hurry down the street. She didn't return to the dog park for Gatsby, and I looked out the window and searched the park. Where was her yellow dog?

"What are you looking for?"

"Gatsby. She was waiting in the park when I got back. Do you see him out there?"

Matt stood next to me, and we searched the park for the yellow Labrador. He tapped my shoulder. "Do you think you can trust her? She admitted to drugging her husband." He maneuvered around and tried to embrace me, and I felt the heat coming off him. His shirt was thin and I could spy his very tanned and massive pectorals, just like the cover of that novel hiding in my bedroom and I instantly thought about that very interesting climatic end to the novel.

"Are you still wearing your swimsuit?" he whispered huskily. He caressed my bare arm, and I suddenly didn't care about Caroline or brownies or the suspicious death investigation because his nearness had ignited a small fire in a very private location. "I'm sorry I didn't walk you home, but I needed to talk to Bob about what the police told him. Can I see it again? The swimsuit?" I felt his hand on my leg, tugging at the short hemline of my dress and his eyes were trying to look down the top of my dress.

"Maybe, but you'll have to take off your shirt first," I said daringly.

He moved a fraction backward and pulled off his shirt in one motion, exposing all those tight mounds on his belly. He carelessly threw the shirt somewhere in a far corner of the room. He absolutely resembled the duke on the cover of that book, and my heart raced. He reached down and pulled one shoulder of my sundress down. I let him. I let him undress me all the way down to my very small bikini. Somehow, indoors, it felt much smaller and riskier than it had in that pool. Then, his large, three tennis ball hands were on me. They were sliding all over the place, stirring up my innards, coaxing out a deep animal hunger I had only read about. We stumbled because Henry nosed his way between us again. I grabbed Matt's hand and pulled him down the hall to the back bedroom. I shut the door behind us so Henry couldn't interfere as we kissed passionately. Matt smashed me against the door and pinned me with his bare, bulging pectoral muscles and I felt my chest ache in response and heard myself literally *gasping for breath* and *begging for more.* Good Grief, this wasn't just a romance, it was an erotic romance!

His hands held fast to my wrists, and his mouth trailed kisses down my chest to the teardrop gemstone I always wore for stress and anxiety, and now for erotic tension. His teeth grabbed my bikini top, and I was sure he was going to pull it off. I wanted him to pull it off. My entire body begged him to pull it off. But he didn't and instead backed off. He glanced over his shoulder at the slider patio door with an expression resembling irritation, or worry. I heard it, too, low growls from Henry.

"Do you think she'll come right back? I thought I heard a knock, but it could have been that crazy dog." He turned his golden tiger eyes on me. "I can meet you back here after she falls asleep." He kissed me, deeply.

But the bonking noise from the glass patio door grew louder. Henry was outside looking in. He kept tapping his nose on the door, his signal. We gasped, half-naked in swimsuits and fully entwined. That large hound dog kept sticking his nose into my business. After another kiss, Matt moved away.

"I'm coming back at midnight," he warned softly. "Do you think she'll take one of her pills? If she talks a pill, she won't know what's going on."

"I don't care if she knows," I told him.

He smiled, he knew he had me. He delivered another potent kiss.

"I have to go feed my dogs. But I'll come back when she's sleeping. Hopefully, she'll take something strong right away and go straight to sleep."

Then, there was a loud noise on my front step, Caroline already returning. We raced out to the living room, and I retrieved my sundress, and Matt retrieved his T-shirt. We quickly put ourselves back together and opened the door. Caroline stepped in, carrying a backpack, and glanced around quizzically.

"What happened in here?" she asked, eyes volleying between the two of us.

I didn't know what to say. Was our fooling around obvious? But I watched where her eyes drifted, into the kitchen, and I turned and saw it. *My beautiful olive tree!* It lay sprawled on the ground, roots up, with the empty pot tipped sideways and the soil scattered across every inch of the kitchen floor.

"Oh, Henry!" I declared, as he strolled into the living room and plopped onto his favorite area rug. "What did you do?"

Caroline took two sleeping pills because she claimed she hadn't slept since the police questioned her and her husband disappeared. She feared Eric was lurking in the shadows, watching her, because things were moved around in her house and she sensed a hostile presence the previous night. Earlier, she went to the dog park, hoping Eric had taken Gatsby there, finally calmed down and ready to talk, but neither Eric nor the dog was anywhere to be found. She thanked me profusely for my spare room because she didn't know what to expect when Eric finally returned. Sometimes his mood was better, but sometimes he was worse. Caroline just wanted to sleep in peace in a place safer than her own home.

"I was wrong to add sleeping pills into the brownies," Caroline said with weary eyes. "But you don't know what it's like sometimes. And he always became much worse when… Mrs. Bennet knew just how to push his buttons."

She helped clean up Henry's kitchen mess, even duct taping the cracked pot. Who would have guessed that plastic pot would crack? Then, she disappeared into the guest room, already droopy-eyed and dragging from her pills. I glanced at the clock. Only one hour until my midnight rendezvous. I wanted to shower and shave my legs and put on the sexiest lingerie I could find.

"Hopefully, someone will finally notice my expensive underwear," I said to Henry. "Whatever you do, please behave tonight," I begged him. He looked like he would consider it.

# Day Nine

## with Henry

Just past midnight, instead of Matt in person, I got Matt on the phone.

"I'm really sorry about being late," Matt said. "But I came out to Rick's Dessert Diner to get you something sweet, and the line was extremely long. And my car wouldn't start, can you believe it? I'm waiting for my uber right now."

"I don't want anything sweet. I want you," I whispered, feeling drowsy from the sun and the alcohol earlier. I had nodded off on my king-size bed waiting. Under a demure robe, I wore what most might call a risqué ensemble of lace and satin that hid almost nothing and accentuated everything. I purchased the ensemble during that last relationship, for my twenty-four-hour engagement. My fiancé happened to be an ultra-intelligent doctorate candidate in physics with allergies to dust and pollen and small talk. His body had been thin and pliable, neat and uptight. I was extremely attracted to the fact that he was astronomically smarter than me, like my father. We dated for two years of my graduate degree and most of his books had taken over my study desk, and I thought that was okay. His books were brainier than my books. I bought the risqué ensemble to celebrate our two years together and because he gushed that he recently purchased a diamond ring and planned to present it to me on the following Tuesday, December 5, on what he called the Heisenberg Certainty Day because I would certainly know how he felt about me on Tuesday. He laughed at his own funny joke. Tuesday came, the proposal came, the ring came, the fancy dinner came, then we returned to my place where I donned my very out-of-character risqué lingerie and sauntered into the bedroom to put the cherry on top of our special night. But he didn't even notice. His thick glasses already lay on the nightstand, and he snapped off the light because we both had an early morning the next day.

"You are going to love Rick's chocolate decadence cake. I'm going to feed it to you in bed, and if any crumbs fall on you, I'm going to kiss them away." His voice sounded husky. "I hope you're a messy eater Sarah, because I can't wait to lick it off of you."

*Good grief,* my mind flashed on that erotic scene of Maggie and the duke's picnic tryst, where the duke "cleaned" up a mess of splattered wine that led all the way down to her...

"That chocolate cake sounds very delicious," I swallowed. "I may have gotten too much sun today and feel a little drowsy. If I happen to drift off, please wake me up for that cake. I'll leave a door unlocked."

But I didn't want to leave the front door unlocked. What if Caroline's husband was out there, lurking. I left the back slider door unlocked. Both of them. I noticed that it was raining outside, a light sprinkle. I glanced at the igloo and wondered if I should banish Henry to the backyard for his bad behavior earlier but decided against it. I didn't want him bonking his nose on the bedroom slider at an inopportune time. I was determined to see this erotic romance through, why should Grace get all the benefits? I wrote a little post-it note and put it on the front door for Matt, so he wouldn't go away when he found the door locked.

*The back door's working again. I'll be waiting for you. Sarah.*

I nodded off again. But sometime later, the fiddling of the sliding door woke me. It was the wrong door, the kitchen door. It took a moment to settle my dizzy head. When I finally sat up, I heard the most frightening sounds a person could hear in the middle of the night. It reminded me of a short story I once read. Something about a dark and stormy night, with a maid screaming, doors slamming, and shots ringing out.

Actually, Caroline screamed, a door did slam, it was the bark of a dog that rang out, but it was dark and stormy outside. There were shouts and crashes and cursing, and I was sure a small boy was growing up in Kansas somewhere, but that wasn't what frightened me the most. I heard a noise that sounded like wood hitting flesh and an agonizing voice warning someone to stop doing something or they would be very sorry. I wasn't particularly brave, but I ran to the kitchen anyway, terrified of what I might see. I flipped on the light.

Henry stood on the top of the kitchen table overseeing the situation. Caroline held the small River Cats souvenir baseball bat I stashed in my spare room and swung it inefficiently, hitting George Johnson, who was crouched with his arms protecting his head. They each froze in the sudden light and looked at me, stunned. Then, they looked at each other and stared, shocked. Caroline was the first to move. She backed up, dropping the bat, breathing erratically, her eyes appeared red and groggy, drugged.

"Oh god. I thought you were Eric." Her eyes narrowed at George. "Did he send you to scare me?"

George Johnson was chuckling. Henry growled at him, but George stayed happily amused and surveyed me with a twinkle in his eye. George straightened up slowly, glancing between Caroline and me. He seemed confused and pleased at the same time. I could see that she hadn't really hurt him. He rubbed the back of his head while grinning at me in his leering way. I caught sight of my keys on the floor, near the far corner of the kitchen. How had they gotten there? Why were my keys in the kitchen at all?

"Did you break into my house to get the pharmacy key?" I accused. "I'm calling the police."

"No, no, don't do that. I wasn't looking for a key. I was looking for you." He laughed under his breath.

Caroline glanced at me. She seemed slightly disappointed.

"You really get around," she mumbled.

"What?"

George smirked and took a step forward and I realized that I wasn't wearing my comfy overlarge sleeping shirt under my untied and open robe. I was wearing that risqué lingerie. *Good grief!* I closed my robe as quickly as I could and glanced up in time to see Matt stepping into the kitchen. I would say, his face took the award for most confused and utterly stunned that evening.

Then, there was a fistfight. Henry barked in support, and I finally found my cell phone to call the police. Luckily, a police cruiser was right down the street and arrived in under a minute. I invited Officer Shane Bane inside to break up the now messy wrestling match on my chocolatey kitchen floor.

George sat with zip-tie cuffs on his wrists, and Matt stood against the far wall in the corner with his muscular arms crossed over his chest. Caroline and I were both on the couch, side by side. Henry lay on his area rug, relaxed. Officer Bane stood to one side with a notebook and pen out, looking at each of us like we were very naughty children.

"He broke in, and I'm pretty sure he was after the key to the CSV pharmacy," I told Officer Shane Bane.

"Oh no," George said. "The door was open. I-I was coming to see her," He pointed at me. He smiled mischievously "She's been giving me the eye for days, flirty. She left a note on the door, on a little sticky. It's in my pocket here, look, go ahead and read it." George leaned toward the police officers.

Bane blinked at him without much of an expression. His partner reached over and pulled the note out of his shirt pocket. *Good grief, that stupid note*! I must have been very groggy to think putting a note on my locked front door would only be read by Matt.

"The back door's a joke between us. The dog broke it when we had our first kiss. Seriously, she was waiting for me. If you saw what she's wearing under that robe, you'd know."

"That note was for Matt. The lingerie is for…"

Every male eye in the place stared at my robe. You'd think they had x-ray vision by the way they were looking at my body. Officer Shane Bane recovered rather quickly and set his eyes on his little notepad. Matt shifted gloomily against the wall, staring at me, upset. I could smell the sugary chocolate aroma from the crushed and smeared cake wafting from the kitchen.

"You kissed him?" Matt asked softly.

I shook my head. Caroline's eyes were still groggy.

She chuckled sleepily, "Everyone said you were shy."

George grinned, shaking with his restrained laughter, but Matt was still frowning. Henry shifted noisily and stared at Officer Bane. I pointed to George.

"He was after the key to the pharmacy. He wants drugs. He tried to pass a fake prescription last week. He used a fake name just like Mrs. Bennet did. But we caught it right away because it wasn't in the system. I think he wanted my key to get his drugs."

That wiped the grin off George's face. His complexion turned extremely red in a matter of seconds.

"That is a lie," he growled. He glanced at Matt. "Isn't it obvious? She played us both for fools and is embarrassed because we showed up at the same time. I'm sorry, man," he said to Matt. "She had us fooled with her nice, angel girl act, right? We're idiots. She's after a backdoor man. Did you notice the new doggy door? I don't think Henry *or Josh* is going away anytime soon."

Matt flinched as his sad brown eyes flicked between us, then to Henry. I shook my head at that terrible, awful, red-headed liar. Officer Bane put his notebook away, but George kept talking.

"Let's see her prove anything. Do you have the *fake* prescription, doctor? Any record in the pharmacy of me being there? I don't think so." His eyes glittered at me. "Don't worry, I'm not upset that you played us both, and I'm still willing to be your back door man if Matt craps out on you, you obviously need it. We just need to keep our signals from getting crossed." He smirked.

Caroline rolled her eyes in disgust, and Matt fidgeted. Officer Bane nudged George with a thick boot toe. I could not face that police officer. For some reason, I felt ashamed in front of him, like I was a very naughty girl and he was an honorable boy scout helping me sort through my messy web of indecent appointments.

"Hold your tongue, Mr. Johnson," he snapped. "So, you want us to charge this one for entering uninvited?" He indicated George. He pointed to Matt, "What about that one?"

"That one's okay," I said meekly, embarrassed. "He was invited."

But Matt did not look okay. He looked disappointed at finding George in my house, and I wasn't sure he quite believed George was only after the key to the pharmacy back room. The police took George away, and Caroline began groggily cleaning my kitchen floor for the second time in one night. Matt stood at the door with a furrowed brow, staring at Henry's furrowed brow.

"Is that Josh guy going to be upset at us when he picks up his dog?"

"He might be a little upset," I admitted. "Matt, I'm not attracted to Josh, not like I am to you. Josh and I barely know each other, and I already let him know that it was over between us." *In a text*, I didn't add. I was indeed a terrible, terrible person.

Matt still looked unsure. He must be thinking things over. Good grief, he was thinking about the mess in my house, the non-chocolate-covered mess. I felt suddenly anxious and grabbed my teardrop gemstone. He didn't need to tell me the mood was shot on our midnight meeting. The events of an hour ago had killed any anticipation of that erotic adventure. Plus, it was close to three o'clock in the morning, and I was practically comatose on my feet. We said our goodbyes for the night, and I traipsed back into my bedroom, dejected. Henry followed me. As I climbed into my king-sized bed, Henry climbed into his doggy bed. We stared into each other's eyes for a long time. I still wore that fancy lingerie under the sheets. At least this time someone had noticed.

"Oh, Henry," I said softly. "Maybe I should just stop making wishes."

I joined the morning crowd in the dog park. I had been neglecting Henry's needs and wanted to make it up to him. Plus, in the morning, there was no evil eye from Isabella to avoid. She was an evening dog park person. Henry and I didn't have much time left, and I dreaded the moment Josh would come and take him away. As I sat alone on a bench, watching how cute Henry's tail wagged as he sniffed in the shade, my phone buzzed.

"Rumor has it that the mysterious death investigation is ending, which is good news for us." Doctor King sounded relieved. "It should also take care of our little problem out here in the pharmacy, help us close our investigation, too, so hopefully we'll be up and open in the next few days."

"Oh, good," I said. "I was worried that it'd take longer. That's a relief because half the people around here think I might have poisoned Mrs. Bennet. Did they say what killed her or who they caught?"

"Not to me. The police were pretty hushed mouthed."

"Have they recovered the items from her last big pick-up?"

There was a short pause. "You mean the Eleanor Vance stuff?"

"No, the bigger order. The one you filled the day before. The one with the *Dracula* and *Frankenstein* names."

There was a short pause. "Oh, did the police mention those items specifically? Did you tell the police about that order or any of those names?"

"I think I only mentioned the Eleanor Vance name," I said. "They can get the rest out of the system anyway, right?"

"Right," he said. "Look, Sarah, this is very sensitive for us, and the pharmacy. Please don't say any more to anyone, police included, not without our representative present. If they want to ask questions, make them do it at the station. We have our own investigation going on, and the police need a warrant to access the data bank and the information we have. We are legally obligated to do things by the book. We have to protect the privacy of our customers, don't forget your oath."

"Oh goodness, sorry. Okay."

As soon as I hung up, the phone buzzed again, this time with an unfamiliar number.

"Hello?"

"Hi, this is Stan, a friend of Josh's. Is this Sarah?"

"Yes. Hello, how are you?"

"Fine," he said. "Josh said you might be having problems with Henry. Lots of people have problems with Henry because Henry is a very stressed-out dog."

My eyes locked on that large hound relaxing in the shade. He certainly hid his stress well.

"He has abandonment issues. Not Josh's fault, Henry was a rescue dog and came with those issues, and Josh's new travel schedule doesn't help. I think he got Henry before thinking it through. His schedule isn't the best for taking care of a dog. Usually, we help each other out with our dogs, but this time I had New York and Josh had Japan at the same time. Long story short, I can come to get him if you'd like. Troy said you wouldn't give him up."

"Troy wanted to put him in a crate."

There was a short pause. "I like you already for not allowing Troy to put him in a crate. That would have been extremely stressful for Henry. Did you figure out his little secret?"

"His secret? What secret? Henry has a secret?" I stared across the granite runway at the hound dog with a secret.

"He can't be closed off. Henry doesn't like to be cut off from the person he's with. He needs to be able to get to you or he'll go nuts. Did you figure it out? Keep the door open, that's the trick. Let him have a way to get to you. If you leave him alone, make sure he's able to wander in and out of every room in the place, everywhere, even outside. If he feels closed in or shut out, he'll act out. He's a trained bloodhound, you know. He can't be closed in."

So, that was the secret of Henry: keep the door open.

I thanked Stan for his call but declined his offer to fetch Henry. We only had one more night together, and I couldn't let him go yet. Stan chuckled over the line and said he knew just how I felt. Henry was an easygoing, caring companion, as long as you knew his secret. For some reason, Josh never let that lesson sink in. When I ended the call, I noticed Matt entering the park. He closed the gate and began walking toward me. He didn't have his dogs with him, so he had come to see me. Another man followed him over, and I overheard that man asking about the police search the previous day. I could see a pink patch on Matt's cheek, roughed up skin from his late-night scuffle with George. Matt must be thinking terrible things about me.

"Scotty has a nephew at the station," the man told Matt. "Said the kid admitted to quitting Mrs. Bennet because she didn't pay him, and the boy said she was making him do too many odd jobs that he didn't want to do anymore. Dog stuff. He allegedly stole all her money and ransacked the place looking for drugs."

"She was robbed?" I suddenly asked.

The man nodded. "Apparently. The boy claims there should have been more pills at her place. Scotty thinks Micah poisoned her tea, killed her, and took all the money and pills."

Matt was unusually quiet as the man prattled on with his insider information. Matt watched me with pensive eyes, and my anxiety inched up again. It was probably too late for us; he didn't trust me. George's poison got into his system. That thought hit me as a moment of clarity overcame me. *George!*

George must be the one who had ransacked Mrs. Bennet's house! It had to be George. He wanted his drugs, *Erythropoietin and Hydrocodone,* for training purposes. He failed to get them with his fake prescription and said that Mrs. Bennet was holding out on *him.* He seemed desperate for those drugs. But why would he still need my key if he ransacked her house? Did he not find them? Something wasn't adding up. Hopefully, Officer Bane told the detective the events of the previous night and what I reported. After the man left, Matt plopped on the bench beside me.

"Sarah," he blurted. "I've been thinking about last night. Let's start over and have a dinner date, alone, just you and me. I'm so sorry about yesterday. I drank too much at that pool party, and I was very forward. I was a little drunk, and your swimsuit made me a little crazy." He looked embarrassed. "And I guess I've been acting a little like George. We got into kind of a competition about you and I rushed things wanting to beat him. So maybe we should slow down. It'll give you time to clear things up for good with that guy, Josh."

My goodness, he still wanted to see me!

"And I bet Caroline is still staying over at your place," he said. "Is she still there?"

"Yes," I said. "She asked to stay until she knew her husband's temper settled down. She doesn't want to stay at a hotel. She says it will add fuel to the fire if she spends money like that. She's pretty certain he will be calmed down after all this time, but she won't know for sure until he shows up again."

Matt nodded. "It looks like this investigation is ending, too, so that'll ease things up around here. Why don't we go out and have a nice dinner date tonight and do things right? We can forget everything about last night. My sister always told me to give a girl three dates to make up her mind before getting physical like that, and I didn't give you your three dates yet. Ice cream can count as one, tonight we'll have dinner, two, then when Caroline is out of your house, and you've settled things for good with Josh and Henry, we can go on a third date. Maybe then you'll give me a better look at what was under that robe. I barely got a glance."

Soon, Matt had to go. A friend promised to give him a ride to the repair garage for his car. I was suddenly happy again. As he ran off, I watched Matt's messy long hair and large hands. I wondered why I liked him so much. I worried that it was only lustful impulses at his sexy body and handsome face, but he was more than that, right? Matt seemed to be a nice, sweet, standup man. He was brave, and vulnerable, and honest, and he wanted me to be honest, too. *Honest and honorable*, like the duke! Henry moseyed over to my bench and put his large head on my lap and stared up at me.

"Oh, Henry," I said. "I might have another chance with him. Isn't that grand?"

Grace arrived with Mollie a few minutes after Matt departed. She skipped over to sit with me as I adjusted Henry's collar. I decided to add my teardrop lepidolite stone next to his nameplate. If Henry suffered from abandonment stress, I wanted to help him. That stone could be my farewell gift to him. I hoped Josh would let him keep that teardrop mineral on his collar. *Good grief. Josh.* I was not looking forward to seeing Josh, but realized Matt was right. I should solidly clear the air with Josh as soon as possible, in person, in a dignified way.

"Did you hear? I got a call. The investigation is coming to an end. I'm allowed to leave the state now." Grace rolled her eyes. "But they didn't tell me anything else."

Grace massaged the top of Henry's head with me.

"Matt just left, and that fellow down there told us all about the conclusion of the investigation," I said.

"So, you and Matt?" Grace raised her eyebrows.

"I think we're very interested in each other," I told her shyly. "I just wish I knew more about that ex-girlfriend up in Washington. Do you think he's still heartbroken over her?"

Grace shook her head, chuckling. "Oh, no. His sister Lola told me that he despises her. When he dropped out of firefighter training, she continued with it and wasn't supportive of Matt at all, or something like that."

"Oh," I said. I hated that George's words sprang into my mind. That man was complete poison.

"So, if you're now interested in Matt, does that mean you are no longer interested in that fellow Josh?"

"I thought you already had a friend with benefits."

She laughed. "It's an ex-husband with benefits. I'm sorry to say, I still drop in on him from time to time, which makes it hard on our bitter divorce. We have a love-hate relationship, emphasis on the hate, so I need to move on. I'm intrigued by your friend, Josh. He looks like a nice guy with a good job, but only if you're not interested in him. Maybe you can introduce us. He's more like a friend to you, right?"

That might be a nice way to end things with Josh, introduce him to someone else. I told Grace that Josh was due to pick up Henry the very next day, sometime in the late afternoon, close to the dinner hour. Perhaps she would like to be there when he showed up. Then, Henry and I went home to do some yoga before my dinner date with Matt, and Grace started her dog park calisthenics.

Even though Doctor King advised against it, I called the detective at the end of my workout to reveal what I knew about George Johnson. They needed to take all the information into account before reaching any conclusions regarding that boy Micah. That kid was very young! I wondered if they searched George's residence for any missing drugs.

"Did Officer Bane report what happened at my place last night?" I asked the detective over the phone. "I wasn't lying about George Johnson. George said that your people know about his attempts to obtain certain substances, but I wanted to be certain of it. I know your people are winding down your investigation and have everything pinned on Micah. Micah drugging the tea and..."

"We know Micah didn't drug the tea or take any drugs from that house," the detective cut me off. "Look, a lot of unusual stuff went down at Mrs. Bennet's house, and we've pieced it all together pretty nicely. To put your mind at ease, we know Micah had nothing to do with the drugs found in any of the food items and someone else's fingerprints were all over that teapot. But Micah did do a few other things, and that's why he's in juvenile detention. Other than that, I cannot tell you more about Micah. And don't worry, you've never really been a true suspect in this investigation."

"George Johnson. Was it George's fingerprints on the teapot? I heard him that morning outside my house, he was planning to drop in on Mrs. Bennet."

"I can't reveal whose fingerprints we found," the detective said. "But let's just say you need to be careful of the people you invite into your home."

"He wanted certain drugs. If his fingerprints were on that teapot…"

"Gail Bennet did not die from anything found in her teapot," the detective interrupted me. "Yes, she certainly set herself up for quite a fun tea party, but none of those substances were in her system or caused her death. Mrs. Bennet had an injection site on her neck. Someone made a clean injection into her jugular with a high-level poison, it only took a minute for her to die. It looks like a professional job. I can't tell you more than that, except to assure you that all your neighbors have been cleared and are no longer suspects, including Mr. Johnson."

I felt like I was processing slowly. She was poisoned by injection? Not by anything she ate or drank?

"Have you searched George's house, though? He used a false name, George Wickham and I'm certain Mrs. Bennet picked up the very pills he wanted, the very next day under the name John Seward. And from conversations I overheard, I gathered that he felt Gail was overcharging him for those pills."

"We know about Mrs. Bennet's clients. We know about that one, but you say she picked up an order the previous day for *John Seward*? Would you like to make another statement? Do you have more to add? Any more names we need to know?"

"No, I don't have any more to add," I said. "It should all be in the data system at CSV."

The detective sighed. "Please put your mind at ease, Doctor Fitzgerald. We are seasoned professionals here and are not going to arrest the wrong person. This looks like a drug-related gang hit. Gail Bennet stole a lot of business from a rival gang recently."

There was a fancy Korean restaurant near the Barnes and Noble booksellers and Target shopping center. They cook the food right at the table on small gas grills. The food is spicy and sweet and tangy all at the same time. Matt ordered short ribs, calamari, and mixed vegetables. We ordered Japanese beer and talked about that funny Netflix show Henry and I didn't watch the other night. Matt told me everything I missed.

His ex-girlfriend, the firefighter, was getting married in October up in Washington, and Matt's sister received an invitation to the wedding. He claimed to be okay with it, even happy for her, but he wouldn't have gone anyway because he wanted to get back into the firefighting world before seeing all his old friends again. They would be happy he was no longer floating along with that awful event hanging over his head.

"It sounds like they blame you for getting burned," I said.

Matt's eyelid fluttered. What was this? Did I hit a nerve?

"Everybody has their own opinion," he growled. "I suppose a few people believe I should have done things differently and that… But that's all water under the bridge now, and I'll show them. I'm going to start training as soon as I can. That situation is done and gone."

He must have seen my questioning expression.

"You know how it is. Something goes wrong, so someone must have done something stupid. Like what happened at your work, right? How could anyone possibly blame you for any of that business?" he argued. "And with me, something similar happened. How could anyone point a finger at me when a hundred different factors were affecting that situation? But I let that chief make me feel like it was my fault, and I dropped out of the academy. And people followed the chief instead of thinking for themselves. If you ask me, that's wrong."

"Of course," I said.

"Speaking of work. I'm glad the investigation is coming to an end. Have you heard if the pharmacy is going to open again?"

"I got a message that says very soon," Then I told him everything the detective revealed earlier. "I wish the police would tell me which substance they found in her system. I'm curious. Isn't it crazy how many different types of drugs she had in that house, all mixed into the foods and drinks, but it was something entirely different that poisoned her?" I shook my head. "Did you know Caroline was convinced her brownies may have played a role in Gail's death? Caroline confessed to the police that she put sleeping pills in the mix and didn't understand why they never arrested her. I'm relieved that the police realized it wasn't Micah's fault. He's too young to be in that kind of trouble."

Matt leaned over the table with a look of absolute happiness on his face.

"I agree. Can I tell you something?" He appeared very relieved, smiling handsomely, chuckling. "I need to get this off my chest. For a minute there, I was certain I might have been responsible for Mrs. Bennet. When I dropped in that day, she asked me to fill the teapot back up. I took it into the kitchen and added hot water and...I also added in *sugar*."

I stared at him.

"You added sugar to the teapot?"

"I didn't know. I usually make iced tea, and I add sugar to the pitcher. I thought I was supposed to add the sugar to the teapot. Stupid, right?"

"Right," I said, not looking at him.

The rest of the date went by in a blur. I kept thinking about the fingerprints all over the house and the fact that Mrs. Bennet hid her drugs in plain sight in a sugar bowl. Did all those fingerprints belong to Matt? Matt continued laughing and flirting with his tiger's eyes, no, his asbestos eyes. *Stop it,* I told myself. The police searched his house and didn't find anything, nothing. But something about him didn't feel the same anymore.

He pulled my hand across the table and kissed it.

*He would let Caroline believe her brownies killed Mrs. Bennet.*

He poured me more beer and topped off my water glass.

*He allowed George to accuse Grace of poisoning Gail with scones.*

He smiled with his straight white teeth and said I was one of a kind.

*He quietly let the police blame a small boy for making a toxic tea.*

He kept babbling through dinner, but he must have sensed my reserve. His voice faltered, slowing slowly, from happy to flat. On the drive back to my house, he began to appear worried. He walked me to the front door, watching my every step. He stood a couple of feet away from me, quietly staring at my face.

"What's wrong?" he asked softly.

"I don't know," I said. Matt was not half as cute without the smile. In fact, he no longer appeared cute at all. He looked like an overgrown messy boy.

"The police say she was injected with something, you told me that. So, it wasn't the tea that killed her. I didn't do anything wrong."

"I have to think."

"Don't bother," Matt snapped. "There's nothing to think about." He turned around and stomped away.

My deflated mood slowed my movements and I entered the house feeling down. Henry lay on his area rug, and Caroline sat dozing on the sofa while the television flickered quietly. She confessed to taking two sleeping pills again because she needed to sleep, and then trudged off to her room. I wondered if I should also take a sleeping pill. Instead, I sank onto the small area rug with Henry.

"Oh, Henry, I'm so confused. I don't know what I need," I whispered to him. Clearly, Henry believed I needed a giant hug and walked over to lay his heavy head in my lap. How did he guess? I only needed him.

# Day Ten

## with Henry

*I* felt mired in a deep sleep under the spell of an odd and unsettling dream. A faraway dog barked. Scuffling noises echoed in the background that sounded like people dancing badly, stepping on each other's feet and bumping into walls and arguing about it. A cavalier Matt was saying that he did nothing wrong, and a supine Josh insisted that he had done nothing wrong, and Henry turned out to be an old man with short gray hair telling me to be careful of who I invited into my house while staring at me under a very furrowed, hound dog's brow. Then, I heard the bonk, bonk, bonk of Henry's signal.

I shot up to a sitting position, disoriented and groggy, struggling to see in the dark. Henry's doggy bed was empty, and he was not in the room. My bedroom door was closed, and the bonk, bonk, bonk persisted. I glanced at the slider door and noticed Henry's silhouette outside. Did he forget about the doggy door? I dragged myself up to let him in.

Henry ignored his cozy bed and crossed over to my closed bedroom door instead. He began thumping his nose on the wood. Something about that closed-door chilled me. *Who shut my bedroom door?* I opened it gingerly and peeked into the hall. Something was amiss. The air seemed to stir but the hall was empty and dark. Then far, far away, I heard a strangled cry that might be a cat, or maybe a woman in distress. Good grief! That kick-started my pulse. I stepped further into the hall and noticed that my front door was wide opened. Now my pulse raced.

I stood rigidly in place, but Henry was not so cautious and meandered right down the hall to the front door to bark. I followed tentatively. *Had they released George Johnson? Or had Matt come back, angry?* I noticed that my armchair had been moved out of place. I noticed Caroline's bedroom door was ajar. I pushed that door wide open and saw that the entire room was askew. The bedsheets scattered, the desk chair on its side, and knew that her husband Eric had found her.

"Caroline?" I whispered, as I poked my head into the room. I flipped on the lamp and searched all around. The room was empty. "Caroline!" I called back into the house.

But the house stayed silent and dark. Henry inched out, onto the front step, sniffing around. He glanced back at me before slowly inching off the stoop and onto the walk. He wanted me to follow him. Good grief, Henry! Low-level stratus clouds obscured most of the moonless sky, and I peered desperately into the very dark darkness. The light from the streetlamp in front of my house barely touched the fence of the dog park. I took up my cell phone and dialed the police but was instantly put on hold and hung up. I dialed Officer Shane Bane's private number, as it was still at the top of my recent calls list, thank goodness.

"Something happened at my house. My guest is missing."

"What?" His voice was groggy. "Doctor Fitzgerald?"

"My houseguest is missing, and my front door was cracked open," I said. "I think her husband found her, and I'm concerned about her."

I heard shuffling over the line. "No one is watching your side of Natomas tonight," he said. "They pulled us off the watch to focus on south Natomas."

Something got knocked around on his end and I realized I must have interrupted him in a deep sleep cycle. How rude of me.

"I'm sorry, it's my day off. I'll call the patrol on duty to head toward your house, but they're probably in south Natomas, and it might take a while unless you call 911. Is it an emergency?" he asked. "Just stay put, and stay safe, someone will be around."

"Okay. It doesn't feel like an emergency."

I hung up, then I immediately heard something in Regency Park. A muffled cry, *stay away.* Henry sniffed and walked toward the sidewalk periodically turning his head back to me. He waited for me to follow him.

Couldn't Henry see that it was pitch black in that park? I couldn't see a thing under the new moon, and the voice out there did not sound happy. That was surely Caroline out there running and hiding. *Was it an emergency?* What should I do? What if her worst nightmare had come true and her abusive husband found her and violently chased her into that dark park? Or maybe they were just arguing. I felt jumpy and impatient and reminded myself that I wasn't responsible for Caroline's awful marital choices and had no way of helping her anyway.

I spotted the forgotten can of pepper spray sitting on my narrow side table, unused and ready for action. The can contained two percent by mass of tear gas, mixed with hot pepper agent, and the stream supposedly reached up to twenty feet, and it was able to *make a grown man cry.* At least, that's what the words on the can advertised.

I grabbed the can of spray, a leash, and the hoody Caroline had left on my sofa and ran down to Henry at the edge of my yard. He gazed at me with sad eyes, his large nose sniffing comically in the air. Henry was a trained bloodhound, Stan had bragged. I offered the hoody for Henry to sniff.

"Can you find her?" I asked the large dog. "Are you a real bloodhound?"

In answer, Henry put his nose to the ground and started moving at a steady pace across the street right toward the darkness. I followed along, tethered to the leash, and clutched my can of mace. The police might take too long for Caroline. One good punch took less than a second, and she'd have another black eye, or a broken nose, or maybe something worse. Her fear in my kitchen was real, she was convinced her husband might beat her badly. Now he was probably playing hide and seek with her in that extremely dark park, ready to pay her back for a chocolate-sweetened deep sleep. I had never been considered a stupid person, but I was pretty sure my current actions would be classified as extremely stupid.

Henry didn't require any light. He followed his nose. He meandered, then bolted, then meandered again. He strung me along, going fast, slow, fast, slow. We passed the caged dog run portion of the park and walked deeper into the blackness. The grass cooled the atmosphere, and the air felt thicker and foggy. We followed the footpath past the elementary school, crossing over the curvy paved walkway. Henry pulled me toward the bend of the large L-shaped recreational park. The dark pressed down on us, and I wondered if someone knew we were out there and if those breathing noises were just Henry and me, or someone else, too. My paranoia heard footsteps everywhere and I felt eyes on my back. Henry pulled me toward the rough area, the drainage weeds and the spillway. I almost stumbled on the uneven grass. We were headed toward the short tunnels below one of the small bridge walkways. As we approached, I could see a dark mass in one of the three holes, something or someone crouched along the wall. It was Caroline, shaking with either fright or cold. Her eyes were wide open, and her hair was a tangled mess. I passed her the sweatshirt still clutched my hand, and she pulled it on.

"Did you see anyone?" she whispered.

"I didn't see anyone," I whispered back. "Are you okay?"

"Please be quiet and get down. You'll draw him here."

"It's okay, I brought mace. We should go back to my house."

Henry barked and jumped, but there was an awful sounding thump and a whimper from Henry. A couple of more thumps, and Henry began whining and crumbled to my feet. In the dark, I didn't see any of it, but I quickly realized that a fat shadow had kicked Henry more than once, and the dog puddled to the ground on his side.

"No!" I shouted. I sank to Henry and checked his floppy ears and neck, thank goodness he was breathing.

Then, I saw him, a broad specter in the darkness, more sinister than the mild-mannered man at Swabbies. The whites of his eyes glowed in the dark, and I growled at him, and he called me a fowl name. He lifted one large leg and kicked me right in the head with the bottom of a heavy steel-toed work boot. I literally saw stars, then I saw nothing at all. But I heard everything.

A scuffled struggle. A couple of harsh slaps on flesh. Then, came a diatribe of very offensive misogynistic words mixed in with more slaps. I could not believe my ears, how extremely rude! The nerve of that man and his mouth. Then, a weak pleading voice followed by a thick accusing voice.

"You think you can do that to me?" A deep male voice rasped.

"I'm sorry." Caroline's crying, gasping voice responded.

"You think you can hide from me?" The deep voice.

"I'm sorry, I—"

A loud slap rang out. "Do you go cryin' to these women about me? Do these people know what I have to put up with, you drugging me? And then you drag these stupid—"

And then came the sound of aerosol spray. *Streams up to twenty foot.*

Followed by the sound of screaming, hellish pain. *Two percent tear gas.*

Topped off with the sound of a heavy mass stumbling and whimpering to the ground. *Able to make a grown man cry.*

I finally managed to sit up and noticed my vision had doubled, but in the dark night, it didn't much matter, and I felt unusually calm. I was able to gather Henry onto my lap. He kept whimpering but he seemed to be breathing okay. Maybe that man broke one of Henry's ribs with that steel-toed kick.

Caroline crouched over the man, using up the last of that can of mace on his face. He squirmed, still cursing and screaming bloody murder between gasps. What would we do when he recovered? There was no way I would leave Henry lying in that dark park next to that awful man. He spluttered out more of his offensive words and stood wobbly on his feet. Why did I believe a can of mace would be enough to stop a violent man?

But Henry stopped whimpering and sprang forward, sinking his teeth into a leg, above a leather boot. The man screamed and tottered backward into the night. Henry growled and went for his butt. I heard rapid, uneven footsteps moving away. His shadow disappeared into the night, and Caroline helped me stand.

"I'll help you get home," she said softly.

All three of us stumbled toward my side of the park. I was no longer so cross-eyed and noticed Caroline had taken more than one fist in the face, her left cheek looked swollen and blotchy. Henry walked funny but seemed okay, and I patted him on the head. The dark silent park felt sinister, and I expected Eric to jump out at any moment, like a crazy killer in a bad horror movie. What if he returned with a weapon, a chainsaw, or a poisoned apple? I searched my pockets but my phone was MIA, probably lying in that dark ditch. I should have called 911 before going into the park, but I didn't know that it would be a real emergency.

As we approached the fenced dog run, the street light cast a welcome sphere of light to guide us home. Caroline still held me around the waist, and we moved awkwardly together. My face did not feel good and the back of my eyes ached.

"Was that Eric?" I asked softly.

"He's not always like that," she answered just as softly. "I'm sorry he hit you. I tried to lure him away from your house. I don't know how he found me."

Caroline hesitated and then I noticed the car. Someone was sitting in a nice Mercedes Benz under the light outside my house. Her body language was not frightened, and I realized she recognized the person in the car, then I recognized him. Doctor King quickly emerged from the sedan and hurried toward us.

"Oh goodness, what happened?" He helped steady our walking. "I knocked, but no one answered. I had no idea..." He was looking at Caroline. "Was it Eric again?"

She nodded. We made it to the porch and sank to the steps. Doctor King looked over Caroline's bruises, then me, then Henry. He searched into the night, and I'd never felt so happy to see anyone before. Thank goodness for Doctor King!

"Doctor King?" Caroline asked softly. "You remember the brownie recipe you gave me? Well, I baked it for Gail Bennet the other day. Do you think I could have poisoned her?"

"Oh, no," I glanced at Caroline. "The police said it wasn't anything in the food."

The doctor patted Caroline's hand. "Don't fret, Carol, those brownies wouldn't kill anyone," he assured her. "Why don't you go inside and rest? I'll stay here and keep watch." He shooed her away. "Go on."

Doctor King pulled out a packet of Motrin that he gave her and advised her to take one of her pills. Caroline wearily slipped into the house, her movements were laggard and slow. When she disappeared inside, the old doctor released a long sigh and then regarded me with serious eyes. It suddenly struck me as strange to see Doctor King outside my house in the dead of night. What was he doing here?

"He's a terrible man, her husband," he said. "Forced her to quit working at CSV last year because he wanted to keep her dependent on him. I wrote out that brownie recipe a long time ago, the first time she came to work in an obvious way. She's not a bad girl, just stuck."

"Doctor King, why are you here?" I felt my pulse quicken.

"I think you know." His eyes flicked back to the dark park, and his eyes search all around. "It's about the false names. We need to keep quiet about the names you saw in the system because… I erased them." He looked me right in the eyes. "To cover up my mistake. I admit it, I added orders to the computer for her. I didn't think she was lying, and that office is always late and glitchy. They often forget to input an order. But if this gets out, it could completely ruin me. I lost everything a few years back, and I can't lose my reputation, too. Right now, the police only know about Eleanor Vance and possibly one other name they found on a container at her house. I erased all the rest. As far as anyone knows, we did not let drugs go out unethically. She was only able to get the one bottle of painkillers from us, a long time ago. We can survive that, but not the rest of it. We supplied a large drug operation, and we'll go down in flames if it gets out that I allowed those handwritten notes to get through. So, our story needs to stay small, and you're the hero here. You caught her."

"But what about that large order she picked up the other day? Weren't they searching for those drugs, what if the police find those pills? They'll track them back to CSV."

"They're not going to find them," Doctor King said.

Who was this man with the thoughtful eyes under those bushy brows? A million questions rushed through my head, and I wasn't sure what to do. Did he just admit to knowing where those missing pills were hidden? And if he knew the whereabouts of those pills, did he… I didn't want to finish that thought. I noticed Henry's eyes perk up. He could feel my unease.

"Look, this can be settled very easily," he said. "Eric hated Bennet for trying to help his wife last year. I know all about it. Bennet gave Caroline a safe haven and encouraged her to file a report against Eric. Maybe Eric killed Mrs. Bennet out of hatred, a plausible scenario. Caroline went to the Bennet house the day she died, maybe Eric followed her there and killed Gail Bennet. Everyone knows that woman recently did something to set him off. And then maybe he came here wanting to do the same to you, for interfering. Look at you, and Caroline, and the dog. He definitely assaulted each of you, so it's not a stretch to say that he tried to kill you, too, but failed and ran away." Doctor King nodded and gave me a small smile. "Think about it. We can rescue Caroline from her abusive husband and clean up our own mess in the process. We wouldn't even have to invent a story. We could just nudge the police in the right direction. It would tie up everything. Our little problem will be solved, Caroline's little problem will be solved. It's a good outcome for everyone involved. She deserves to be free of that maniac."

I didn't understand a word he was saying and must have appeared extremely confused. Doctor King inched back to give me some space, and I wobbled to my feet.

"Sarah, I am appealing to your better nature here. We can really help Caroline. This is the perfect opportunity. Like Mrs. Bennet, he's not going to stop. That woman did not want to return those drugs or the bottles, and she tried to blackmail me into…" He closed his weary eyes for a moment and pressed a finger and thumb on the bridge of his nose. "We can erase our mistake, believe me, this will solve everything."

Good lord, *our mistake?* I went to my door and held it open for Henry, but Doctor King pushed Henry aside and moved quickly. The doctor slipped into the door, pushing me deeper into the house, then closed the front door firmly, shutting Henry outside. He locked it and spun around to face me. His expression was as pleasant as it had been the day he complimented my glowing California tan. On the other side of the door, Henry bonked his nose, his signal.

"I don't know what you're asking me to do," I mumbled.

"Eric came here to retrieve his wife and he was angry," he said softly to me. "You tried to stop him, and he hit you, and he hit her, and he hit your dog. All of that is true."

Doctor King pulled a latex glove from his pocket and slipped it over his hand.

"He tried to kill you, Sarah, but he was not successful, and he ran away. It's a perfect conclusion, just say you'll go along with it."

He pulled a plastic syringe from his breast pocket. The needle was still covered with a plastic cap.

"He left this behind. This will tie him to Bennet's death. This is the best outcome for all of us, Sarah. Please, this is the best outcome."

His eyes pleaded with me.

"He's a terrible man. A terrible man."

I stared at the syringe in his hand. *Doctor King had come to my house in the small hours of the night with a dose of poison in his pocket.*

The detective said that Mrs. Bennet died in less than a minute. I was very curious to know the ingredients in that little tube of plastic. Which chemical poison did he use? Did he special order it? I stared at it, wanting to get a closer look while at the same time knowing I should scream and run away. I remained frozen in indecision, partly because I still could not bring myself to believe that Doctor King, absent minded hummer of disco music and teller of bad jokes, was a killer.

Plus, Caroline was in the other room sleeping, and she needed her sleep. I noticed that Henry stopped bonking on the door. Where had he gone?

"What do you have in there?" I asked softly.

"Will you go along with the plan?" His voice sounded hopeful.

"Did you actually kill Gail Bennet?" I finally said it out loud.

His face changed into a mask of disappointment and anger. He was no longer the nice old man who puttered around the back pharmacy room chuckling at me and bringing me chocolate treats. In this face mask, he was a stranger, and strangers meant danger. Doctor King pressed his lips together in an expression of severe dismay. His voice came soft as a whisper.

"I gave you a chance, Sarah. I didn't want Eric to be successful, but you leave me no choice."

He took two quick steps toward me and stretched out his free hand. One thing about long hair that never came up on the pros and cons list of whether to finally cut it short… it is very easy to grab. Lots of long strands everywhere, and once a person has hold of a good clump, it is a snap for them to move your head, and of course, the rest of a body follows the head.

Doctor King took tight hold of my hair and directed me to the sofa, the dog watching sofa. He violently flung me into the overlarge soft cushions. He wasn't a very good murderer because at this point, only my scalp felt a bit sore, my cushiony sofa was a soft hit and hardly frightening at all. It was difficult to accept that he meant to kill me after landing on such fluffy pillows. He pushed me down with a flat hand, strong against my struggles, but more determined rather than mean. He did not strike me and I completely expected him to renege on his decision to poison me. He used his body mass to hold me in place and all the time held the syringe up high in one hand, to protect it from my flailing arms. I noticed he did not look at my face, and he began to hum under his breath, "Staying Alive," his favorite song. I stared right at him, but he kept his eyes on my neck.

I wondered if he killed Gail Bennet in a similar way. Did he throw her onto that soft bed, refuse to look into her eyes, and then stab her with the needle trying not to hurt her? Did she also wonder if he was just kidding? It struck me as a little comical, but I needed to remind myself that Gail Bennet was dead, and in a few minutes, I would likely be dead, too. Good grief, I needed to muster up the right frame of mind for fighting him off.

As my eyes went to the arm that held the needle, a low growl erupted behind the doctor. I watched the large jaws of a hound dog clamp onto Doctor King's wrist, and as that arm was yanked down, the syringe flew out of its grip. Henry launched a full-on attack. Henry dragged the doctor into the kitchen, the mass of them wriggling across the floor. I could see blood dripping from the doctor's arm as Henry pulled him to the back doggy door. Doctor King kicked and swung his arms but could not seem to make contact with Henry until one big kick. That kick succeeded in separating Henry's jaw from Doctor King's arm and sent that precious doggy head banging against the wall in a terrible way. Doctor King rolled over exhausted, and startled, and he looked like the old man I once knew.

But I would not be fooled again because when he kicked Henry, it kick-started my fight response. I quickly grabbed the roll of duct tape on the kitchen counter and bound his legs up at the ankles, then I quickly duct-taped one arm to the kitchen table and I bound his bitten arm to his body, securing the appendage and stemming the blood flow all in one move. I knew he looked ridiculous, but I did the quickest binding job I could before running to poor whining Henry.

"Oh, Henry," I whispered into his big floppy ear. "Please be okay."

The police arrived fifteen minutes later with Eric in the backseat of the squad car. He had been casing my front door from the dog park. The cops stared quizzically at the old doctor duct-taped to my kitchen floor, startled to see him there. Caroline woke, and one of the officers drove us both to the emergency room to treat her sprained ankle, fat lip, and bruised eyes and my minor concussion, but we were released right away. Henry suffered rib damage, and the vet prescribed him an anti-inflammatory with pain killers, but his prognosis looked promising. He just needed lots of care and rest. I was grateful to Officer Bane for rushing Henry to a twenty-four-hour emergency vet. He hadn't even been on duty but drove across town to my house directly following our phone conversation. Officer Bane arrived sometime after the arrest and before our ambulance sped off, but he instantly took charge of Henry, alleviating my anxiety. By the time I returned home from my hospital visit, Officer Bane and Henry were sitting on my porch in the early morning sunlight. Officer Bane wore a college sweatshirt and sweatpants, and appeared tired and droopy-eyed. I sank beside him on the porch to stroke Henry's brow.

"Oh, Henry, you look wrecked."

"The vet says he's going to be just fine." Shane Bane passed me Henry's medication and papers. He shot me a small smile. "What about you?"

"I'm going to be fine, too," I told him. "I'm not sure about Caroline. What do you think is going to happen with her?"

"I don't know." He let out a long breath. "But for the time being, her husband will be behind bars for assaulting you two in the park. She could get a restraining order."

Officer Bane left us to get some sleep, and Henry and I took a long nap together, in the master suite. Him on his doggy bed and me on my king-sized bed. I stared at that hound dog for a very long time before drifting off. I didn't know how I would survive giving my dog back to Josh.

The rapping on my door woke me up, and I found Grace standing on the porch looking quite pretty. She brought over a bottle of wine, and I invited her in. I had forgotten all about her request to meet Josh. She entered quickly and went over to the window to spy on the dog park. I glanced outside and watched most of the afternoon crowd. I spotted Matt on the far side, throwing tennis balls for the dogs. He wore a sour expression and glared periodically at my front door. It was hard to believe I had found him so irresistibly attractive a short time ago. What had I been looking at?

"I heard all kinds of crazy rumors," Grace said. "Are any of them true?"

I nodded, "I'm sure a few of them are true."

"Which ones?"

"If there's one about Caroline being chased in the park by her husband in the dead of night, it's true. And the one where Caroline emptied a can of mace on him, also true. Or the one where Doctor King might be a murderer, I think that one's true, too." I looked back at the park. "And the one where Matt and I are no longer interested in each other. Absolutely, positively true."

"Good God, that's crazy."

"Not that crazy. As it turns out, he isn't exactly an honest man."

"Matt? Or the doctor?"

"Both," I said.

Josh's shiny new Lexus rolled up. He jumped out carrying a bunch of flowers and a gift bag. He wore nice slacks and a button-down shirt. His tie was a little loose, but not one hair on the top of his head was out of place. I glanced at Grace, and she seemed nervous.

"Maybe this is a bad idea," she said. "He looks like he's hoping to woo you."

"This is a perfect idea, maybe he'll woo you instead." I opened the door before he had a chance to knock.

I invited him in. He seemed surprised to see Grace standing there opening a bottle of wine. I accepted the flowers and put them in a vase, avoiding the kiss he tried to deliver. Pretty soon, we all stood drinking wine as I relayed the harrowing night Henry and I survived. Josh stood with his mouth agape, either surprised at my story or that I was doing all of the talking.

"He's in the backroom sleeping," I told Josh. "I think he should stay here and rest, right where he is. The pain killers have made him a little groggy."

We went into the kitchen to sit, and Josh noticed the doggy door. He noticed the igloo on the back porch and the torn-up yard. He studied me quizzically.

"You want me to leave Henry here?" he asked. "I thought he was being naughty."

"He was," I said. "He was very naughty. He marked the whole house that first day. And tore up the yard, and destroyed my screen door, and tore off the knob in the bathroom, and flooded that whole room. He ate a small corner of my yoga rug and the couch cushion… and he probably killed my olive tree." I frowned at that last one.

Josh was wincing, and Grace was giggling.

"But he had his reasons," I said. "And I think one of his reasons is that he wants to stay here, with me, indefinitely. We worked it out, Henry and I. Please let him stay with me, Josh."

"Does this mean you aren't breaking up with me?" Josh asked, confused.

"Oh, no, I'm definitely breaking up with you," I told him. "We both know that we won't work, not as a couple. But we can be friends, and you can visit Henry anytime."

Josh furrowed his brow, not unlike Henry, and looked to Grace for help.

"She got hit on the head last night." Grace smiled at him. "I can't see why else she would want to break up with you."

Josh finally noticed Grace's striking beauty, her flawless skin with dark charcoal features and sharp chin. His eyes widened at her. Josh agreed to let Henry stay a few more nights to recover and give him time to ruminate over my proposal. I told them I needed to rest and recommended they eat at that Korean restaurant across from the bookstore. Josh obviously arrived hoping for a dinner date. He could take Grace instead, I insisted, as she was dressed for dinner, and, I was not. I stood at my front window and watched Josh and Grace chat in an animated way as he helped her into his convertible car. She must be relaying events of the past week because his eyes were wide with astonishment. They sped off, looking absolutely right together in that fancy car.

# More Days

## with Henry

Josh agreed to allow Henry to stay at my house for a couple of days as he recovered, which quickly turned into a whole week. That week bled into his trip to Texas because he needed a sitter, and when he returned, he allowed Henry to stay with me indefinitely, which meant forever. Henry was now mine, and I was now Henry's. Josh visited us once a week, but Henry and I both knew that his visits were just a ruse. He really wanted to see Grace. He timed his drop-ins when Grace brought Mollie to the dog park. Then, we noticed the visits happened when he walked with Grace and Mollie to the dog park from her house, both dressed for dog park calisthenics.

Not long after the Bennet affair, the CSV pharmacy reopened for business with a new lead pharmacist. A tall, skeletal-thin doctor from a nearby CSV pharmacy volunteered to oversee the operations. Doctor Vitale never hummed anything while he worked, he just pressed his lips together and tsked. My duties shrank to part-time, which was fine with me because classes were due to start soon and I needed to seriously shop for a car.

Matt's sister returned to sell her house and Matt immediately moved away, making a point to say goodbye to everyone except me. On the flip side, George rode his bicycle past my house in a blur every day and waved when he saw me as if we were old friends. Isabella still flashed narrowed eyes at me whenever Henry and I entered the dog park, but she always meandered over to gossip about everyone in the park. Caroline returned to her own home but rarely came around. The rumor mill reported that her husband was still in jail and her dog was mysteriously missing.

One afternoon, as Henry and I strolled into the dog park, we noticed another hound dog laying in the shade. A dog who could pass for Henry's identical twin. I spotted Officer Shane Bane sitting on Mrs. Bennet's bench. He smiled and waved at me expectantly. He was dressed casually in a simple polo shirt and shorts with clean tennis shoes and athletic socks stretched over his shins. He looked a little bit nerdy, but handsome and clean. His hair was very disciplined. Between his thick fingers, he held a thick tattered book that appeared to be a science fiction fantasy novel. *He likes true fantasy fiction*, just like me, though his genre was science and mine was romance.

"Hello there." He waved to me. "We decided to try your park today hoping we might run into you two. There aren't many pure-bred bloodhounds around here and I thought they might like to meet each other."

Henry and the other hound immediately began their sniff tests.

"O'Henry, this is Catherine. She's also a trained bloodhound. Catherine, this is the hero hound dog I told you about. His name is O'Henry." Shane spoke to the two dogs as they happily circled each other.

"O'Henry?" I stared at him.

"Isn't that what you call him? I thought I heard you call him O'Henry a couple of times. Isn't that his name?"

"Henry, but yes, I guess I do call him O'Henry." What a nice new twist to his name, I loved it. We watched the two hounds wander around together, sniffing all the different parts of the park. Henry had never done that before. Maybe he just needed a friend to share the smells with. Shane and I exchanged glances and chuckled at how the dogs went right off together, fast and instant friends.

"It's a match! They are getting along! Catherine has never taken to another dog like this before." Officer Bane grinned excitedly, beaming. He had clearly been worried about his hound dog finding a friend. "They like each other!"

"I think they do," I agreed.

"I guess that means we should probably let them get to know each other better." His friendly eyes turned to me. Honest, intelligent, neat, handsome, and he emitted an old-fashioned, calming aroma. That was how I would describe Officer Shane Bane. His nicely muscled arms and hands were tipped with neatly clipped nails. He was a conscientious man.

"We have a dog park in my neighborhood, but Catherine hides from all the other dogs there. I'm glad I brought her here to meet oh… Henry," he said. He laughed, "Look at them, I think it's true love."

I spied down the granite run at the two dogs strolling and sniffing happily together and realized something. *Good grief, wasn't there a Henry and Catherine in Northanger Abby?* The summer romance I wished for way back when I first moved across the country was meant to happen after all, just not the way I first imagined it. Those two canines were destined for a classic romance and a sweet happily ever after. I chuckled and smiled at Officer Bane.

"Definitely true love," I said to his twinkling eyes. Then, my eyes locked onto his strong jaw line as I recalled the feel of his arms when he carried me into my house that evening. A flood of warmth cascaded down my limbs.

*Oh, Henry, I think we are in for another adventure here.*

# The End

# Acknowledgments

*Thank you to my husband Bob and Sparky for being the special inspiration for writing this story. All I wanted was to make up a story in which the "Bob" character was right on the money about some conspiracy…unfortunately, the Bob character in real life did not want Bob's theory to be right and that made for a better ending. So, Bob was right after all.*

*I also want to thank my girls, Jonna, Annie and Grace Batten for the support and encouragement they deliver on a regular basis. Their insights are always valuable and Grace's idea that Sarah should end up with Henry was right on the money.*

*Thanks also to Whitney Morsillo for editing my final draft on short notice -all while on the verge of giving birth!*

♥

# About The Author

*Joanne Alain Cook* is a mother, wife, sister, teacher, artist, officer, and writer. She currently resides in Northern California with her very sweet and handsome husband of 20+years, her beautiful brainy daughters, a goofy Labrador, an angry bearded dragon, three frightened chickens, and a school of clueless fish. Find out what she has in the works at joannealaincook.com.

Other Books By Joanne Alain Cook

Read the exciting *Spectral Analysis* Trilogy! It's more than just ghost story, jam packed with sci-fi, pagan, mystery, and romance.

Part 1 – *Spectral Analysis* A fractured past, entwined with a new inflamed desire, is the perfect combination to aid skeptical Janine into believing the paranormal…but will her enlightenment occur in time to subvert a tragedy?

Part 2- *Spectral Voices* As fate forces her to face some startling mystic abilities, Janine grapples with how she fits into the greater scheme of things, all while facing unresolved feelings for the man she scorned.

Part 3 – *Spectral Redemption* An ancient curse, reeking of passion, betrayal and murder, force Janine and Kiki to question the men they love, all while ominous events send them spiraling towards a deadly conclusion.

9 781737 589259